DEDICATION

This book is dedicated to my husband, with much thanks for his willingness to share his love of history with me. Had it not been for him, I would not have spent a hot and muggy day of family vacation driving around Gettysburg while listening to a cassette tape that explained the entire three day battle in great detail. I would not have gotten out of the car time after time to walk in the footsteps of the various regiments. And my life and my understanding would have been greatly diminished.

This book is also dedicated to my three valiant sons, who, despite the heat of the very long day patiently walked Pickett's Charge with their parents, then beat a hasty retreat back to the car as if followed by grapeshot and canister.

CONTENTS

CHAPTER ONE
THE CROOKED TREE

Sarah Jewell McCoombs glanced between her Ma and Pa. Ma's arms were folded tightly across her apron front. Pa studied the dirt under his fingernails. Sarah stood a log on its end and sat down. In a McCoombs' family argument, patience was a virtue.

While she waited, Sarah watched her little brother, Lijah, crest the little knoll that forced Plum Run through the rocky vale behind their neighbor's farm. He carried a misshapen chair leg from Pa's scrap pile against his shoulder like a rifle. The blond cowlick on his forehead fanned the air like a cockade. Beside him, Daisy's tail waved like a regimental flag. It was all very patriotic, but it irritated Sarah. This family had given enough to the war effort, what with Micah being gone and all. And the nation had seen enough death. Why did Lijah have to play the soldier? And why did Ma have to pick on this little tree?

Pa cleared his throat. "Don't the Bible say wait seven years before you cut down a tree for being unfruitful?"

"John McCoombs!" Ma snapped. "The Good Book ain't no farm manual."

"I 'spect so Martha. Still, it's a shame to cut it down without giving it a chance."

Sarah studied the scowl on her Mother's face. Once Ma made up her mind, she closed it up as tight as the cellar door in a squall. Ma said weeding out the sickly was the nature of things. Like the last time Daisy had pups, and Ma told Pa to smother the runt. He'd argued, the pain in his tear-filled eyes making Sarah's insides hurt. Pa lost that argument. Sarah hoped he wouldn't lose this one, too. The tree was the only thing on the whole farm more crooked than she was.

Ma let out a long, exasperated sigh then craned her neck back to look in her husband's face, towering a good foot above her own. "Five years with no fruit is chance enough. Besides, the way it leans, it's going to heave over in a storm someday. When it takes out the side of your carpentry shop, then who'll be sorry?"

Pa stroked his beard. He gave the tree the same ponderous look he gave steers at the Pennsylvania State fair.

"It'd make a good climbing tree when it gets a little bigger." Sarah interjected. Ma scowled at her and Sarah felt her face flush. She tugged at her back brace, then studied the tip of her sandy blonde braid, just as Pa had studied his fingernails.

"You ain't built for climbing trees, Sarah Jewel," Ma said. "An' your brother would find no joy climbing a tree this crooked."

Ma's words cut into Sarah's stomach even worse than the brace did. She flipped her braid over her shoulder and studied the eastern horizon. After days of unrelenting rain, the rising sun was burning the haze off the ridge. This evening, when she sat down to write in her diary, Sarah would note that Monday, June 15, 1863 was hot and humid.

Pa brought his hand down from his beard and stuck it behind the strap of his overalls, patting his chest the way he did when a decision was made and he accepted it.

"All right, Martha. The tree will go," he said in a voice that sounded as determined as his wife's. "If Micah was here, I 'spect I'd have it out today. But best save the tree for later and get done the things what's pressing first. Sunrise this morning was pink as a baby's bottom. We got a piece of rough weather ahead. "

Sarah felt herself relax. The tree wasn't safe, but Pa had postponed its death sentence. She watched her Ma chewing back bitter words as Pa ambled out to the far field. Ma never thought anything was more pressing than what she declared needed to be done.

Ma whirled on Sarah. "What is it with your brothers and soldiering? Ever since Micah ran off to join the Army, nobody's done a lick of work unless I kicked up a fuss. Go tell Lijah to stop marching and start hoeing. Then get to your books. You can't be lazy if you 'spect to be a teacher soon."

"I don't 'spect to be a teacher. I want to be a farmer's wife, like you," Sarah said as she struggled up from the log.

"Who's gone marry you, warped like you are?" Ma stomped to the chicken coop and pelted the pullets with cracked corn. The grains nearly planted themselves in the scratch-softened soil.

Sarah lit out for the knoll before Ma had a chance to hurl a handful of grain at her. Ma'd done it before, and it hurt worse than hailstones. Besides, she didn't dare tell her mother that she knew who would marry her. Not since even he didn't know it yet. When Martin Snyder had left for war, he'd thought of her as no more than Micah's little sister, but that was going to change. Sarah could picture how he would come back from the war and notice that she'd grown into a fine, straight woman. He wouldn't notice the bulky lumps of the brace beneath her dress. All Sarah had to do was wait until the war ended and Martin came back. Then everything that was askew in her life would be put to rights.

Sarah bent to examine the woolly, gray meadow sage that sent up its sweet, musky scent when her long skirts brushed against it. Her mother chopped its oblong leaves for seasoning Sunday pork roasts and stuffing, but Sarah assumed the herb must be good for more than just cooking. Though most of her studies bored her, she had learned enough Latin to know that its real, scientific name, Salvia, meant healthy. Sarah knew that Dame Heatner, who lived out near Power's Hill, knew which herbs made good teas and which made poultices. People called upon her in times of sickness. But Ma was skeptical of such things. Ma said Dame Heatner was a crazy old crone, her knowledge nothing but old wives' tales, folklore for the uneducated. Better, said Ma, to trust to modern medicine.

Sarah stood back up, gasping for air. The brace cut into her skin. Its straps pulled her shoulder blades back so they almost touched each other. It made sleeping difficult. Every week Ma tightened the strap which ran down her left side, forcing her right side to stretch out, evening the height of her shoulders. The strap that wrapped around her waist kept her from shrugging the whole contraption off, but it cut off her breathing when she bent over or sat down. She tugged at it, but it was under her clothes and fastened behind her so that she could not loosen it.

"Lijah! Throw down that stick and go help Pa in the far field. Gettysburg will be safe from the Confederate Army without you."

Lijah dropped the stick and bolted. Sarah held Daisy by the collar and watched his head bob through wheat taller than he was. Most of it was still green. Here and there it had turned almost as golden as his hair. It would be ripe for cutting in a few weeks.

While she watched him go, Sarah picked aimlessly at the brace and wished that Doctor O'Neal had never noticed her warped back.

Sarah's misery began the previous December, on a day when she came in cold and wet from her outside chores. The chill did not leave her, even after she stripped off her sopping mittens and socks. Her shawl steamed as it hung by the fire to dry, yet the marrow of Sarah's bones remained as frozen as the pond in February.

Ma said that this was not something to be ignored, not with all the troops moving through the countryside, bringing their terrible pestilences with them. More boys had died from measles and pneumonia than from bullets. Ma rubbed Sarah's clammy feet between her hands to warm them. She boiled strips of cloth, wrung them dry, sprinkled them with turpentine and draped them on Sarah's chest to draw the chill from her lungs. It wasn't pleasant, but Ma said it was always effective.

Until now.

After two days, when Sarah's rattling cough set Daisy to howling, Ma called the new doctor, fresh from Baltimore and full of modern ideas, who put his ear to Sarah's back and listened. Mother wanted some new patented medicine, but Doctor O'Neal announced that there was nothing wrong with Sarah that a little comfrey tea and some more time in bed wouldn't fix.

It was then that Sarah made the mistake that robbed her of her future and her comfort. The doctor was standing in the doorway, explaining how to make cough syrup from horehound, ginger, and licorice root when Sarah got out of bed to fetch the throw that had slipped to the floor.

"Mrs. McCoombs, will you look at that," Doctor O'Neal said.

Sarah snatched up the throw and spun around, holding it up to her chin.

"Sarah Jewell McCoombs, you crawl back into bed this instant," Ma snapped.

"No," the doctor said. "Turn around. Now bend, so your hands touch the ground in front of you."

Sarah did as she was told, although it made no sense.

"Do you see that, Mrs. McCoombs? How your daughter's right and left shoulders do not match when she bends over?"

"I see it," Ma answered. Her voice had that suspicious

edge to it, and Sarah knew that Ma thought the doctor was getting ready to sell her something she didn't take much store in; something even stranger than some syrup of horehound, ginger, and licorice root.

"Now child, stand back up, but do not turn around," Doctor O'Neal said in a gentle voice. Sarah stood, facing the wall, wondering what the doctor was seeing that caused such distress. "You will note, Madam, how your daughter's shoulders fall forward?"

"She is lazy. Girl, stand up straight!" Ma barked the order out, reminding Sarah of the sergeant when Martin Snyder marched off to war with the 87th Pennsylvania Infantry. Sarah stood as erect as she could. She threw her shoulders back until she heard them pop. The Doctor clucked his tongue.

"This is very grim. Your daughter, Madam, has a scoliosis. And a kyphosis as well."

Scoliosis and kyphosis. Sarah didn't know what the words meant, but she didn't like the sound of them. She repeated them. The sounds slithered over her tongue like sinister adders foretelling doom. Ma took a sharp breath at the sound of such scientific words. The doctor's cough remedy had not impressed her. Scoliosis and kyphosis did.

Later that night, Sarah listened to Ma talking to Pa. She was warped, Ma said. She might never carry a heavy load, nor bear children. She might even die while still a child herself.

Sarah stuffed her fist into her mouth to choke down the sobs. What place did she have on the farm if she could not work, could not bear children? Would she be ripped up and cast aside like a weed? Culled out like Daisy's runt pup?

Scoliosis and kyphosis. Sarah craved gentle words to replace the terrible ones, but she knew she would not get them from Ma. Talking was not something Ma took lightly. It was restricted to directions, to everyday tasks. Fetch your brother. Hoe the garden. Pass the salt. Ma didn't allow anyone in the family to waste words on feelings and fears. Work overcame fears.

Ma said nothing the next morning, nor the morning after that. Sarah began to wonder if the horrible words were nothing but a fever induced nightmare. She refused to talk about them, refused to think about them, but the words kept bubbling up, filling her throat like bile from an upset stomach. How could she live when death crept along her backbone? She tried to banish her fears, but they lurked just out of sight in the dark corners of her mind.

When Sarah was finally well, Ma fitted her with the brace. The strap and buckle device became Sarah's constant torment. It cut into her shoulders. It blocked her air. Worst of all, it reminded her that she was warped and as fruitless as the little apple tree that leaned perilously close to the carpentry shop and, like all things unproductive, needed to be fixed or weeded out.

CHAPTER TWO
THE ORDERLY WORLD

When she was sure Lijah was going straight to Pa, Sarah followed Daisy's flag tail toward the house. She entered the kitchen just as Ma set the copper boiler full of wash water on the stove. Ma did the washing every Monday, rain or shine. She slivered animal fat soap into the pot, stopping occasionally to stir with a big wooden paddle. Ma washed towels and washcloths first, then underwear, nightgowns and socks, Pa and Lijah's good shirts, Sarah and Ma's dresses and finally, when the water was almost too brown to do much good, the muddy work clothes.

Like every morning but Sunday, Sarah's books waited on the kitchen table where Ma had mustered them like soldiers on review. Sarah scanned the spines of the books: Robinson's Arithmetic, Towen's Speller, Frost's United States History, Weld's Grammar and finally McGuffey's Eclectic Reader, stood in order, from right to left, bookended by the kettle and the iron. Ma made Sarah begin her studies with the book on the right and progress right through to the left. She settled gingerly into her chair, trying not to jab herself with the brace buckles.

Sarah leaned over and patted Daisy, the latest in a long line of black and white spotted dogs. With the lone exception of Constance, the sorrel mare, every animal on the farm was either black or white. Ma would not allow Pa to keep any cow except black and white Jerseys. All the pigs and chickens were pure white. Order. It was Ma's way.

"Help me wring these," Ma said, startling Sarah from her musings. Sarah pushed her chair away from the open arithmetic book and the too-clean slate board and turned the wringer handle as Ma fed towels through two rollers, squeezing the water from them. Sarah glanced at the copper boiler just as her nightgown fought its way to the top. It waved one arm at her, as if begging to be saved, then sunk down again.

Sarah heard the Snyders' loose jointed cart rattle by on the Emmitsburg Road. She knew the Snyders' middle child, Hans, who was fourteen-years-old and nearly as tall as his Pa, would be driving. He used to pick her up, back when she and his sister Mary both went to Mrs. Eyster's Young Ladies' Seminary. The two girls would giggle and whisper all the way to school. They were going to be sisters-in-law. Sarah was going to marry Martin, and Mary would marry Micah. But now that she was crooked, Sarah stayed home and Mary went on to school alone. Sarah watched the dust settle back onto the road and wondered why Mary never came to visit.

"Yer lucky there's a war on," Ma said, interrupting Sarah's thoughts. "Back when I was young, women only taught in summer school, when the men-folk was in the fields. Come Fall Term, the district hired all male teachers. But all that's changed since the war. Women teach year round now. And make good money at it. Upwards of eighteen dollars a month."

Sarah applied herself to the crank until sweat ran into her eyes. She didn't want to spend her days huddled over books when she could be looking at flowers and herbs and the way her brother grew taller and more freckled with each new day. She pulled the heavy oak wash bucket off the table. "Let me hang these for you, Ma."

Ma gasped. She held out a protective hand but Sarah ignored it. Sarah already had a good four inches on Ma, so it was easier for her to carry the enormous wash bucket, warped back or no. Sarah lugged the load outside, set the bucket in the damp dirt, and began pegging towels on the line. Her back caught each time she stood up, but it was better than listening to Ma's niggling.

Sarah heard the ching and clop of a carriage. She turned as Doctor O'Neal pulled into the yard. He glanced between her and the bucket. "It is my considered opinion that pegging laundry is not a good occupation for a girl with your condition, Miss McCoombs. And please tell me you did not carry that bucket out here yourself."

Sarah drew circles in the mud with her big toe.

Ma came out onto the porch. She wiped her hands with a towel, scowling fiercely. "Answer the man, Sarah Jewell."

"I did, sir," Sarah whispered.

The doctor clucked his tongue. He took his black bag off the seat of the carriage and climbed down.

Ma stepped aside and let him through the door. She threw a look at Sarah that cut as deep. All Sarah wanted to do was help. "So, Doctor," Ma said aloud as she and Sarah followed him into the front parlor, "why're you here? Ain't no one sick."

"You have forgotten, Madame, that I promised to come in six months to check on the progress of your daughter's spine. I am a man of my word. Today is exactly six months since I last attended her."

Ma took Sarah into the kitchen and helped her remove the brace. When she finished, the doctor asked Sarah to turn away from him and touch the ground, much as he had on that dreadful day in December.

Doctor O'Neal clucked his tongue, a sound Sarah had

begun to associate with doom. "Your daughter's spine is, I fear, as crooked as ever, perhaps worse. We have no recourse but to apply a plaster cast to impede further curvature of the spine. I shall need a hook or a block and tackle sturdy enough to support her weight."

"Hook?" Ma sounded incredulous.

The doctor nodded. "Madam, your daughter's spine must be made as straight as possible if I am to apply a plaster cast to any affect. To do so, we must place her in traction."

"Traction? Cast? What are you planning to do to me?" Sarah's voice climbed with each word. Her heart leaped like a rabbit with Daisy in chase, but there was no place for her to run, no bush to hide behind. The doctor waved her questions off. Obviously, children were to be seen and not heard, even when they were speaking of their own bodies. Ma resolutely crossed her arms over her chest and Sarah knew she had no choice.

They settled on the block and tackle in the barn. While the doctor went back to his carriage for his equipment, Ma stripped Sarah down to her bloomers and camisole. Doctor O'Neal tied his equipment onto Pa's pulley. He slid each of Sarah's arms through a strap loop, then bent her arms up at the elbows so that she held the straps like the ropes on a swing. Sarah gave Ma a relieved smile. This was not so bad.

The doctor then placed a cage-like contraption over Sarah's head and strapped it firmly under her chin. Before she could tell him how awkward it felt, he hoisted on Pa's rope. Sarah's feet left the barn floor. She dangled. Sarah thought her head would snap off. She tried to protest, but her weight pushed her teeth tight against each other. She stiffened, trying to relieve the pressure.

"Pulling up on the arm straps defeats the purpose of traction. And for heaven's sake, quit kicking. You shall break your neck," Doctor O'Neal commanded.

Sarah rolled her eyes toward her mother, but her mother

turned away.

Doctor O'Neal pulled a roll of downy-soft quilt batting from his bag and wrapped it around Sarah's undergarments. He put on a pair of reading glasses and began the fine work of cutting and stitching the batting until it molded to her body. While he worked, he kept up a conversational tone, as if covering hanging girls with quilt batting was as natural as shucking corn.

"Is the McCoombs family planning on leaving?" he asked.

"Why should we?" Ma, who had been looking out the open barn door, turned with a scowl. Sarah saw Ma's eyes widen before she averted them.

"Surely you've heard report that the rebels are coming up the Cumberland Valley. They are using the mountains to screen their movements from Union forces. Governor Curtin sent a telegram just this morning, directing the citizenry of Gettysburg to move its food, fodder and clothing stores as quickly as possible, lest they fall into enemy hands. Most of the bankers and merchants plan to send their goods to Philadelphia for safe keeping."

The doctor rolled layers of plaster-soaked gauze over the batting. He tilted his head back, scowling through the bottom half of his glasses as he worked.

Ma let out a little harrumph. "Rules of war say civilians should be left alone, long as we don't aid and abet anyone."

Sarah knew the rules of war might say civilians and their property were to be respected, but she had heard enough at school last fall to know that rules and reality didn't always square.

"At the very least, Madam, consider sending away your husband, horses, and livestock. He is at risk of being captured and sent south as a prisoner, and I am sure you are aware that both sides conscript good horses and livestock."

Despite the pain roiling down her spine, Sarah chuckled. Any Confederate soldier who tried to ride the swayback, dapple gray Beatrice would look like he was slung in a hammock, rocking along with her lumbering gait. But Constance, the sorrel, was a good enough horse for either army and Lijah would be heartbroken if the rebels took Bossy and Dover, the family's cow and calf. She shuddered at the thought of Pa being taken, and the movement sent a thousand painful jolts down her stressed spine.

"Y'ain't too sure of the gentlemanly ways of your boys in gray, are you?" Ma said.

Sarah gasped. Now wasn't the time to mention that Doctor O'Neal was a copperhead, a democrat who sympathized with the Southern cause. Not when she was so vulnerable.

The doctor snorted derisively. "They aren't my boys, madam."

"You sure? Word is the Democratic Party promised you the patients at the Alms House and the County Prison if you moved to town to support their cause. I hear you're mighty outspoken in defense of slavery. Reckon that's why the Presbyterian Church wouldn't have you."

"All true, Madam. Still, none of that stopped me from attending your daughter last December." He wrapped the plaster tightly. The wet plaster chilled as it set. Sarah struggled to keep her teeth from chattering, which made her neck hurt even more.

Lijah's voice called from somewhere behind Sarah. "Where's lunch, Ma? Me and Pa is hungry. Aaaargh! What are you doing to Sissy?"

Sarah tried to jerk her head around. As she spun, she caught sight of her brother in the barn doorway, his mouth agape and his eyes as big around as fall onions.

"We's fixing her. You tell your Pa to rustle up his own lunch today. Now git." Ma waved her hands like she was shooing chickens. Lijah scuttled away. Sarah heard him shouting all the way to the house, where the screen door slammed behind him. Her brother's rapid staccato fell away, answered by her father's deep bass, and even though she could not hear the words, she found comfort in them.

Ma shuffled her feet. "I don't take to seeing my daughter hanging like a ham. How long's she need to keep this thing on for?"

"Remind me of her age," the doctor said. He was peering up at Sarah through reading glasses, checking to make sure the plaster was smooth.

"Fifteen. Sixteen next month."

"The longer the cast remains in place, the more efficacious. The danger of further curvature should be minimized by the time she reaches maturity."

"She's gotta hang there 'til she's eighteen?" Sarah heard panic in her mother's voice.

Doctor O'Neal scowled at Ma over the top of his glasses. "Physical maturity for females typically occurs between sixteen and seventeen. And I was not speaking of the traction, but of the cast. She must hang here until the plaster is dry. Then she may resume a regular life. But no bathing, no hard labor, no bending or lifting." He pressed down on the pads of his fingers as he clicked the points off. "Nothing which would cause her to crack the cast or dampen it. And certainly no pegging of laundry. Should it come off due to excessive moisture or some other unforeseen event, contact me and I will assess her development and reapply the cast as needed."

Tears sprang to Sarah's eyes. No bending, lifting, or hard work did not sound like a normal life. What was left but her books?

After a while Pa brought in a tray of sandwiches, some of last year's dried apple chips, a stack of oatmeal cookies and a pitcher of cherry cider. He could be right handy in the kitchen. He gathered four stools around Sarah, and he and Ma, the doctor and Lijah had their lunch. Sarah felt like a macabre centerpiece, dangling there in her bloomers and plaster, unable to talk because of the weight pulling on her head. Pa gave the sole of her foot a gentle squeeze. His eyes held such compassion that she wanted to cry. The straps twisted, and her gaze fell on Lijah, who smiled, as if relieved that the sister who loved him still existed under all that plaster. But Ma's eyes jerked away. Her cheeks flushed scarlet. Sarah felt shame of disappointing her mother flood over her once more.

The doctor brought her down soon after lunch, and the family went back to the business of being a family. Pa and Lijah returned to the fields. Ma beat into submission bread dough which had overflowed its rising bowl, then helped Sarah find something to wear. It was not easy. None of her clothes fit over the bulky cast, but Pa's shirts did. Ma turned back the sleeves and pinned a blanket over the bottom half, to serve as a skirt.

Sarah felt like one of the dark people, the ones called contraband, who sometimes passed by. They had escaped slavery in the South and passed through in search of a better life in the North. Most wore cast-off clothing, tattered remnants no better than rags. She had turned her eyes away from them. Now she felt their shame. She wished desperately for a decent dress.

Once clothed, Sarah tried to attend to her studies. The bottom of the cast cut into her thighs when she leaned forward. She dropped her chalk and could not bend to pick it up. She could not get up from the chair without Ma's assistance. She could not even take a deep breath.

At the dinner table, much of Sarah's food ended up on Pa's shirt. It was almost impossible to bring a fork to her mouth without bending at the waist. Ma finally slapped down her own fork in disgust and, with much grumbling, tied a kitchen towel around Sarah's neck. Eating with a bib like a baby made her stomach feel like sour milk. She could not eat much anyway. The cast pressed at her stomach.

That night Sarah plodded awkwardly upstairs, clutching the railing in a death grip as she shifted her weight back and forth and tried not to fall backwards down the stairs. She dropped onto the bed, her toes and fingers tingly with exhaustion. Unable to turn over, she lay there, remembering how she once flipped a turtle onto its back so that Lijah could watch its legs flail. She had laughed, her arm squeezing her little brother close as they squatted on the bank of Plum Run, poking the silly thing with a stick.

It wasn't funny anymore. Nothing was funny. What would Martin do when he saw her? Would he be like Ma and look away in disgust?. Or laugh, as she had at the turtle? Whatever look appeared on Martin's face, it wouldn't be the one she was hoping for. No one could love her now.

Sarah jerked awake late in the night. She had a vague, disconcerted feeling that something was not right. The room flickered with dim light and she realized that something was on fire. She strained to hear the crackle of flame, but all was silent until a distant commotion, like something awry at the Weikert's farm, or the Snyder's, their two neighbors to the south, came to her. Closer, Sarah heard the rumble and jingle of tack. Daisy whined as if afraid of being left behind.

Was Pa harnessing the wagon?

Sarah flailed her arms and legs. She was stuck, just like that turtle. She craned her neck and saw Lijah sleeping in his bed. She wasn't alone.

"Lijah. Wake up," she said, first in a whisper, then louder, then almost in a shout. Sarah bobbed her head up and down, hoping to gain enough momentum to sit herself up. With every bob, her cast iron bed frame thudded against the wall.

Thud.

Thud.

Thud.

Ma jerked the bedroom door open and glared at Sarah, the whites of her eyes glistening in the dark like two warning beacons. She was in her nightgown. One hand clutched her robe closed at her neck. Her hair fell down her back in long, wavy rivulets. Sarah could not remember when she had last seen her mother in her night clothes. Ma was always the first dressed, well before dawn, and the last to undress in the evening. She always looked ready to take on the world.

"Sarah Jewell! You trying to bring the house down?"

"I couldn't get out of bed," Sarah sobbed. "Thought you and Pa were leaving, and me and Lijah were going to be burned alive, and I couldn't save him."

Ma crossed to the window. She laid her forearms on the sill and placed her head on them, looking tired and discouraged. "The fire ain't here, Sarah. It ain't over at the Weikert's neither, nor down at the Snyder's. It's someplace way south. George Weikert come by, says it's Confederates, traveling north, burning as they go. But he got nothing to prove it by. Now you go back to sleep. I'll wake you if something happens."

Sarah rolled her eyes away from Ma and found Pa filling the doorframe. He was so tall his hair skimmed the top jamb, his shoulders so broad he often caught one or the other post as he came through. He crossed the room on stockinged feet. Except for his shoes he was fully dressed. He stood behind Ma, blocking the eerie glow from the window, returning the room to normal.

Ma turned. For a moment Sarah saw her parents look at each other, two silhouettes against the orange sky. Pa put his arm around Ma, tucking her against his massive chest. Ma reached out her arms. They did not meet around Pa's waist. The two came back to the bed and Pa brushed the hair out of Sarah's eyes. His hand came to rest atop her head. Big and calloused, it radiated warmth and comfort down Sarah's stretched spine.

"He will not cause a crooked reed to be broken," Pa said.

"John McCoombs! There you go, misquoting Scripture again. Isaiah said 'A bruised reed shall he not break, and the smoking flax shall he not quench: he shall bring forth judgment unto truth.' " Ma patted the center of Pa's broad chest, then laid her hand atop the one Pa had on Sarah's head, adding her determination to his comfort in a double blessing. Sarah watched a tender smile flicker momentarily across her mother's face, wrinkling the corners of her eyes into a dozen tiny lines, softening her hardened features. The smile was fleeting, but it stayed with Sarah long into the night.

"Morning!" Sweet as a baby bird in its nest, Lijah's little voice woke Sarah. There were still a few lingering stars and the eastern sky had yet to pick up a single stroke of pink or orange when Lijah's eyes popped open, ready to start the day.

"Morning," Sarah replied. She tried to get up. It was just as impossible as it had been last night.

Lijah watched her, his hands on his hips. He tilted his head like Daisy did when she was studying something, then burrowed beneath Sarah's plaster casing and pushed himself onto hands and knees. The lever he created with his own body was enough to get her to a seated position. Lijah grabbed her ankles and leaped out of bed, twisting Sarah around, then he crawled behind her, laid his back against the mattress and pushed on her cast with his feet until she was standing.

Sarah clutched the dresser while her brother clattered downstairs. The blood pooled in her legs and her heart raced to return it to her brain. In a few moments her equilibrium seemed to steady itself, so she started down the stairs. Not being able to look where she placed her feet was heart-stopping. Fear slowed her more than the cast. If she didn't think about what might happen, Sarah could make it.

"Where's Papa?" Lijah asked, his voice plaintive and high.

"Your Pa had some business to attend to," Ma said.

"Constance and Bossy and Dover's with him. Some of the pigs and chickens too. Left us Beatrice, case we need to ride someplace. Ain't so bad. You got less animals to attend to 'til he gets back. Now get going with your chores."

"When'll that be? He ain't gonna sell Dover, is he? Why didn't he say goodbye?" Lijah scratched his nether parts with one hand and his thatch of blond hair with his other. His pants hung on a peg by the backdoor. Ma made him shuck them off when he came into the house since he got covered in mud every time he went out.

Ma pointed her bacon fork at him. "Elijah Daniel McCoombs! When you're tall's me, I'll answer every question what comes out of your mouth. Until then, I 'spect you to do what you're told. Now get, or your breakfast'll be cold before you're ready to eat it."

Lijah hopped into his pants. In no time at all Sarah heard him whistling out in the barn.

"Pa take the livestock out of Rebel reach?" Sarah asked.

Ma stabbed savagely at the sizzling bacon. "I ain't discussing it. No sense getting all riled up over nothing. He'll be back soon enough."

When Hans and Mary Snyder rattled through that afternoon, Hans reported that the fire that had seemed so very near the night before was actually in Emmitsburg, ten miles south and over the Maryland border. Twenty-seven houses had burned, but the destruction hadn't been caused by the southern army. To Ma's disgust, she learned that a citizen of Emmitsburg had accidentally started the fire. Pa had left for nothing.

Pa still wasn't back on Friday afternoon, when Daisy went into a barking frenzy. Sarah went out onto the porch and saw Hans pull his team to an uneasy halt near Ma, who was picking peas in a nearby field. Hans' horses danced uneasily in their traces. Skip, the black and tan coon hound, appeared to dance as he shuffled for balance in the back of the wagon. Sarah stepped back into the shadow of the door so that Hans couldn't see her cast. He and Mary had avoided her ever since she got a brace. What would they think of her now?

"The Rebs invaded town! They're everywhere, Miz McCoombs! Firing guns, demanding food and clothes. Got so scared I didn't wait for Mary to get out of school: just left. Some classmate's family's gotta shelter her 'til ma can go after her. I'm stopping by the house fer supplies, then I'm lighting out like your husband did. We's got things we need to keep out of reel hands, including me! I don't want to be conscripted." He shook the reins and was off again, the wagon rattling south.

When Ma finally came in, she was carrying a basket overflowing with immature peas. "We got nothing to worry about. The rebs are here for the town. They won't hurt us."

Sarah knew Ma was lying. Ma, who never picked peas before their pods were full to bursting, must have picked the bushes clean to keep the Rebels from eating them. Her orderly world was awry.

CHAPTER THREE
BY THEIR NAMES

That evening Sarah let herself drop onto a bench on the porch. She studied the clouds lying low against the western hills, their pink undersides glowing even though their crowns were dark. The cool air felt good against her legs, especially where the cast had chaffed them.

Daisy lifted her head toward the Emmitsburg road and her tail thumped a welcoming tattoo against the steps. Sarah squinted into the gathering gloom at what looked like a misshapen lump traveling northward. It was wider than it was tall and seemed to change shape as it came.

"Hey, there," Sarah called to the lump.

"Hey, yourself," it answered. As it drew into the light spilling from the open door, Sarah recognized their neighbor, Mrs. Snyder. As was usual for her, Mrs. Snyder's hair was drawn up in a tight bun and covered by tatted lace, pinned down with a pair of steel-rimmed reading glasses. But that was all that looked usual. Mrs. Snyder was a wide, meaty woman to begin with, but today she wore several of her dresses at once, adding considerably to her bulk. A covered basket swayed under each of her elbows. Bulging pillowcases dangled from each of her fists.

Sarah's heart squeezed in her chest. If she'd known it was

Mrs. Snyder coming, she would have gotten up and hidden herself away. But now it was too late. There was no way she could get up without attracting attention to her body cast.

Mrs. Snyder dropped her baskets and bundles on the porch. She leaned against the porch railing and sighed, releasing so much air as she sat that she sounded as if she had sprung a leak. "Girl, go fetch yer Ma," she said.

"Ma! Mrs. Snyder's come calling," Sarah shouted over her shoulder, hoping that if she remained still her neighbor wouldn't notice the awful plaster cast.

"Be right out," Ma called back. Sarah and Mrs. Snyder stared at each other through the gathering dark. Neither said a word.

The Snyder farm was the most ramshackle in the valley. The stout woman, who was not known to be a diligent housekeeper, blamed it on bad lungs that tightened to a wheeze whenever she stirred the dust that coated her furniture like November's first snow. Ma said Mrs. Snyder was worn down by a hard master. Mr. Snyder was indeed that. The whole valley knew of his drunken rages, his quick and violent outbursts. Everyone had breathed a sigh of relief when Frederick Snyder had marched off to war.

"You got your whole wardrobe on? Do sit down," Ma said when came out, carrying two teacups filled with steaming tea.

"Beats trying to carry 'em all. Don't want no Rebels stealing 'em," Mrs. Snyder answered. She stripped out of four dresses, leaving them in a heap, then squeezed her girth into Ma's tiny rocker. Ma handed one cup to her neighbor, then climbed into Pa's big rocker. They sat there for a long time without saying anything, their teacups poised just below their mouths as if trying to decide whether to talk or to drink. Finally Mrs. Snyder drained her cup and set it and the saucer on the floor.

"I 'spect you heard my boy Hans left town today. Had to

save the rig and horses from falling into enemy hands." As always, she wheezed heavily.

"My John did the same early Tuesday," Ma answered.

Mrs. Snyder picked up her cup. She put it to her lips, found there was nothing in it and placed it back in its saucer. "I 'spect it was the prudent thing to do."

"'Spect so."

"Mary's still in town. And Frederick and Martin is off in the south with the 87th," Mrs. Snyder continued. Her husband and older son had joined Company F of the 87th Pennsylvania Infantry. Sarah knew there were older children as well, both boys and girls, but as they became old enough to fend for themselves, they left the turbulence of the Snyder farm and went off to find lives for themselves elsewhere. Sarah knew more was expected of McCoombs children. McCoombs children were expected to become strong branches on the family tree, not milkweed seeds cast away on the wind.

The 87th had been involved in a skirmish at Winchester just last week, and no one seemed to know what had become of them. Even so, Sarah wished her brother Micah was with them. Pa forbid Micah from signing on, even when all of his friends marched off with the 87th, so Micah ran away and joined up anyway. He went to Franklin County and enlisted in the 77th Pennsylvania Volunteers, the only unit in all Pennsylvania not in the Army of the Potomac. So instead of serving close to home, in Virginia and Maryland, Micah was with strangers in the distant Army of the Cumberland, which served in the west. Micah's letters came from strange, distant places like Tennessee and Mississippi, and they were often weeks old.

Martin and his father were unaccounted for since the skirmish. Micah was in the Western Wilderness. Sarah pushed back the terrible thought that the next time she saw their names might be on one of those long lists of lost or wounded in The Adams Sentinel or The Gettysburg

Compiler.

"So you're left home alone," Ma said.

Mrs. Snyder laughed, sounding like a fireplace bellows. "Even the fool coon hound's gone. Disappeared after Hans left. I don't know whether he followed the boy or thought there was some hunting going on and followed the sound of the rifles. All I know is, it's awful quiet with everyone gone. I can't abide staying home alone. I 'spect I'll stay here till I fetch Mary home."

Ma nodded. "Wouldn't be neighborly to turn you away."

"Didn't 'spect anything less from you, being good Christians as you is." Mrs. Snyder pulled the day's edition of The Compiler out of her pillowcase, then dragged the little wire reading glasses down from the top of her head. "Hans brought this home with him. Seeing as this was printed before the rebs entered the town, seems downright prophetic. Says here, and I quote: 'It cannot be possible that a great battle between two contending armies can be avoided any longer. It may occur at any moment and in our own county. Let our Ladies go to work at once and prepare lint, bandages and other articles that may be useful in the hospital."

Mrs. Snyder folded the paper with great deliberation. She slid it back into the pillowcase and pulled out a bed sheet. The women tore it into long strips, then rolled the strips up so that they could be used for bandages.

"It were Jubal Early what rode into town today," Mrs. Snyder said.

Sarah shuddered. The Confederate General had quite a reputation.

"I hear he demanded $25,000 in good Yankee money, sixty barrels of flour, seven thousand pounds of bacon and a thousand pairs of shoes, among other things."

"Shoes," Ma said with a little snort.

"David Kendlehart stood next to the General's horse and listened. He said it would be impossible to provide such things, given as how the banks and stores had already shipped away all their goods. So them Rebels didn't get nary a thing."

"Brave thing to do, but I guess that's why he's president of the town council," Ma said. "I 'spect them Rebels'll have to go someplace else to find their shoes."

Sarah looked up at the stars as they winked into the oncoming darkness. Eight miles to the west, where the mountains stood black against the sky, there were as many campfires burning as there were stars in the heavens. Those campfires, she knew, warmed the confederate army. The sooner they went away, the happier she would be.

"Queer dress your daughter's got on," Mrs. Snyder said wheezily. There was nothing catty in her tone at all, and no expectation of explanation. It was observation and nothing more. Still, it made Sarah wish she could shrink into her cast like a turtle in its shell.

"It's John's shirt. My girl don't fit in her own dresses no more," Ma replied.

"Reckon she'd fit in one of mine?" Mrs. Snyder pulled the top dress off the discarded pile. It was a faded brown field dress with black hem tape at the sleeves and hem. It was not fashionable, but it would be serviceable and far more becoming than her father's shirt. Sarah struggled to her feet, accepted the offering with a little nod, and retreated to the house to try it on.

Lijah lay his forehead on his arm. "Beans, beans, beans."

"He don't show much gratitude, do he?" Mrs. Snyder commented.

Ma screwed her lips together. "Enjoy 'em while you have 'em. Come winter you'll be wishing you had fresh green beans to eat." She poked him with her fork. Lijah sat back up and stuffed another bean in his mouth.

Sarah stared her own plate of boiled beans. They had

eaten beans twice a day for four days in a row now and she, too, was sick of them. Usually Ma dried some for use later in soups. She canned them in jars to store in the cellar. But this week Ma seemed intent on picking and eating every last bean as soon as it showed on the plant. Sarah wished Pa was there. He could eat a mess of beans. It was Tuesday and Pa had been gone a week now. She wondered where he was and what he was eating.

It was hard on Lijah, not having Pa around. Most days, Lijah tailed after Pa. The two of them went their rounds, feeding and watering the animals, tilling the fields, doing the numerous little chores that kept the farm running. When field work was light, they worked side by side in Pa's carpentry shop. Pa said Lijah showed real talent with wood, the kind that would grow into real accomplishment if he could just buckle down and concentrate. Concentrating wasn't high on Lijah's list of qualities, and Sarah often found herself finishing off one of his chores so that he wouldn't get in trouble with Ma. For now, though, Lijah had to concentrate on making sure that everything Pa would usually do was getting done. It was a tall order for a small boy, even one who tried his hardest.

The fact that Pa had taken so many animals was almost as hard on Lijah as having Pa gone. Lijah loved all the barnyard critters. It was he who had given them all names. Lijah loved the liquid soft eyes of the cows and the beady red ones of the chickens. He kissed the pig's scratchy snout and the calf's velvety nose. It broke Sarah's heart to see her little brother standing in the field, peering east as if hoping to catch of glimpse of Pa herding his precious animals back over Cemetery Ridge.

Sarah stopped chewing her green beans as Daisy scrambled out from under the table and ran, barking, onto the porch. In a moment her bark turned friendly. Their neighbor, George Weikert, leaned in the kitchen window.

"Don't mean to bother you folks," he said, "but I just

heard Gettysburg's back in Union hands. Buford's Cavalry rode in. The Confederates withdrew. All without a single citizen being hurt."

"Hurrah!" Lijah shouted through a mouth full of chewed up beans. He waved his fork like a banner. Ma and Mrs. Snyder smiled at each other across the table.

"I 'spect I'll have to go fetch Mary now." Mrs. Snyder shoved in another fork full of green beans. She didn't look to be in a rush to hike the three miles into town.

"I'll go," Sarah said. She scooted her chair back and carried her dishes to the sink before anyone could protest.

The closer she got to town, the more Sarah wished she could just turn around and head home. At first she was so excited about the prospect of seeing the cavalry and her school friends that she forgot about her cast. But getting onto Beatrice had been quite a struggle, with Lijah pushing and her pulling while the ever-patient nag looked curiously over her shoulder at the hard monstrosity attempting to mount her. Once on, Sarah squeezed her knees into Beatrice's sides so tightly that the horse blew with annoyance. She couldn't roll her tailbone under her because the cast kept her stiff and upright. Beatrice's lumbering gait jarred her bones and banged her thighs into her cast.

Sarah's fear of rejection was even stronger than her physical pain. Her former school mates knew why she had left school, yet none of them had come to visit. Would they accept her now? She pictured them gaping at her. Would they turn away, ignoring her? Sarah felt like a leper, shunned by people as if her condition was contagious.

Sarah almost turned Beatrice around, but her mother's strong, determined voice seemed to well out of her consciousness. She remembered that she was a McCoombs, and McCoombs keep their promises. She had promised her neighbor that she would retrieve Mary, and retrieve her she would. Sarah jutted her chin in defiance and tried to look as tough as Ma, who would ignore the gaping looks, the rude remarks. Ma would do what needed to be done in spite of her handicaps, and be proud of it. But it was hard. Sarah was not Ma. She hoped she would find Mary quickly and leave before anyone else saw her.

Sarah heard her friends before she saw them. They stood on the brick-paved sidewalk, waving tiny versions of the stars and stripes. They sang to the parade of horsemen that clattered by, their swords and stirrups flashing. Sarah recognized Mary, the Myer girls, the Culps, Anna Garlach, Amanda Reinecher, Alice Powers, Tillie Pierce, the Zeiglers, Irene Weisich among the crowd. Mercy, there were a lot of them. She clucked her tongue and encouraged Beatrice onto the sidewalk behind the crowd. Some of them turned and gave her curious looks, but no one asked why she looked so large or sat so stiffly. They did not move away, yet none of them said a welcoming word either. Sarah felt even more leprous.

Finally, Amanda Reinecher stepped back and handed Sarah an American flag. "You going to come down off that nag?"

"Afraid I'd never get back on," Sarah said with a little, proud laugh. She tilted her chin up, a bit haughtily, as if proud of her condition. Amanda turned and rejoined the singing:

A union of rivers and a union of lakes,
A union of land and a union of States,
A union of hearts and a union of hands,
And the flag of our union forever.

The soldiers cheered, and the girls sang the chorus again. And again. And again. They would have sung more than just the chorus if any of them could have remembered the words, but the excitement of seeing so many handsome men was too flustering. The more they sang it, the more the soldiers cheered and the more everyone laughed.

Martin had been that handsome when he marched away. Sarah remembered how his steel gray eyes flashed with excitement, his cheeks flushed pink with the newness of it all. He had stood ramrod straight and trim within his new blue uniform. He was the handsomest, most dashing young man she had ever seen. He had laughed and given her a friendly hug. He called her by his pet name for her, Sarah Doll, and she blushed though she knew that it was just because she was the little sister of his best friend. Now, even though her handsome nineteen-year-old neighbor was far away, Sarah waved her flag and sang as strongly as the plaster cast would allow. Her song was for Martin.

It was getting on toward evening when Mary climbed up behind Sarah and the two of them started south toward home. Mary rapped the cast with her knuckles. "How's this thing working, Sarah? I wanted to ask, but I didn't want to embarrass you in front of the other girls."

"It's working fine," Sarah muttered. But it wasn't fine. The cast stood between her and Mary, a hard and unrelenting reminder of her body's crookedness. She wanted it off, wanted to go back to school, back to being a girl with normal prospects. She wished she could forget.

Mary pulled her arms tight around Sarah. Her cheek bounced against the hard plaster. "Don't matter," Mary said. "You're still my Sarah inside. I've missed you. Now that the scare is over, Hans and your Pa should be back soon. Maybe even my pa and Martin and Micah! What stories they all will have to tell."

Mary's touch could not reach through the cast, but her words did. Mary was as wounded as Sarah. Both wanted to go back to normal. Sarah felt her heart grow soft and warm inside her shell. She looked up at the stars as they twinkled out of the gathering darkness one by one and comforted herself with the thought that the men she loved - Pa and

Micah and Martin- were seeing the same stars.

CHAPTER FOUR
THE LOWERING SKY

S arah looked up from Towen's Speller. "Do you hear it?"

"Yup. Thunder."

Sarah pushed the book aside and stared at her mother. Last September the boom of cannons had rolled like distant thunder over the hills and valleys between them and Sharpsburg, Maryland. This was much closer and, undeniably, the sharp retort of rifles and the roar of cannons. It had begun at dawn.

Ma looked uneasy. "Sounds like it's coming from north and west of town. General Buford must be putting a rout to the last of the confederates. Nothing to concern us."

Sarah returned to her books. Still, she was uneasy all day. There were times where denial was nothing but foolish.

While most of the citizens of Gettysburg seemed determined to wait the conflict out in their cellars, a trickle of townsfolk passed on their way to relatives and friends in the north and east. Sarah went out on the porch and spoke with some of them. They pointed out flashes of metal glinting along the ridges that ran parallel to each other both east and west of the farm. The McCoombs farmhouse was between two armies.

That evening Mary and her mother dragged the Snyder's piano to the McCoombs' farmhouse atop a sledge they usually used to haul pumpkins in from the fields.

"If I knew you was coming, I could'a sent Sarah over on Beatrice to help you," Ma grunted as they hauled the piano up the front steps and into the parlor.

"Didn't want to be a bother," Mrs. Snyder answered. She collapsed into the settee and wiped her flushed face with a handkerchief. "Paid three hundred dollars for that piano a couple years back. It's Mary's pride and joy. Couldn't let Johnny Reb ruin it."

Ma snorted. "Our place is closer to the fighting than yours. Ain't no safer."

Air escaped Mrs. Snyder's lungs. "The rebels won't bother an occupied building. No one's at my place. I can't abide being there without the men."

Mary shuddered. "The confederates were a raggedy band: shoeless, wearing clothes that would shame a castaway. The family that harbored me fed them and they let us be, but in some of the houses, the vacant ones, I heard they poured molasses on the furniture and broke open feather mattresses."

"Don't pay to leave anything good behind," Mrs. Snyder said. "Mary 'n' me left food on the porch, hoping they'd leave the place alone that way. The Sherfys're gone. Trostles,too. Took all nine of their kids."

"If you all want to leave your farms vacant, that's your'n business." Ma picked up a frayed sock. She slipped the wooden darning egg into the toe and began furiously stitching the hole closed. "We're staying put so John can find us when he comes back. But we need extra hands if you plan to stay with us. Wheat's near ready to reap. Almost done putting up cherries."

"We're not going to just eat 'em like we did with the beans? Keeps 'em out of enemy hands." Mrs. Snyder asked.

"You want the runs that bad?" Ma replied.

"We'll do what need be done," Mrs. Snyder answered with a resigned sigh, though Sarah privately questioned whether she really would. The Snyder farm had been even more rag tag since the men went off to war.

That night Sarah lay in bed listening to the soft breathing of her brother and her best friend. They were comforting sounds, but she was not comforted. Her head whirled with stories Mary had told about her encounters with the enemy soldiers. She tried to roll over. The cast trapped her. Sarah strained to listen to something beyond the comfort of her room. Down the hall, the two mothers murmured. Outside there were no cannons, no crack of rifles: just the trill of the cricket chorus. Still, she did not feel comforted. Gettysburg seemed to be waiting, trapped like she was, unable to escape what was to come.

The waiting turned to watching the next afternoon. Sarah was washing up the lunch dishes when Daisy scurried into the kitchen, her tail tucked between her legs. She whined the way she did when Ma yelled at her and tangled herself in Sarah's skirts. Sarah tried to reach down and comfort Daisy with a pat, but the cast wouldn't allow her to bend. She set her foot atop the dog's spine and rocked it back and forth. It was small comfort, she knew, but it was all she could give.

"Come see!" Lijah shouted, Mary hard on his heels. They were still carrying the hoes they had been using in the bean rows and their eyes glistened with excitement. "There's skirmishers in Sherfy's peach orchard."

Daisy dove under the settee in the parlor, but Sarah followed her brother and Mary to the porch. Perhaps a dozen men ducked through the trees just a few hundred feet away. Some wore blue, others gray and butternut. Sarah watched one shoulder his rifle. A little puff of blue-gray smoke floated up as the rifle butt kicked into him and a pop rent the air. Lijah cheered as if it were a parade. Mary held out a trembling hand and clutched Sarah's warm one. Sarah bit her lip in disappointment. It wasn't at all what she had expected a battle to look like. There were so few soldiers. None of them looked any more serious or gallant than Lijah did when he was drilling with his cast-off chair leg.

"Tarnation!" Ma shouted as she and Mrs. Snyder rushed in. "You trying to get yourselves killed? Get in the house!" Ma's face was flushed with running. It surprised Sarah to see her mother, master of all situations, so upset over such a small skirmish. A handful of men, a few rifle pops. She seemed to be over-reacting.

Ma herded them into the parlor and pulled the drapes closed.

"I wanna see," Lijah protested.

"Minie balls are flying out there." Mrs. Snyder's voice was high and tight. Her breath rattled out of her constricted throat. The sound of it made the hair stand up on the back of Sarah's neck. Maybe this skirmish was more frightening than she thought.

"Minie balls?" Lijah said.

"Bullets," Mrs. Snyder clarified. "They hit you whether you're a solider or not. Your ma and I had to lay down amid the rows to keep from getting shot. We could hear them whizzing overhead. We'd be laying there still, but a man nearly stepped on us. He told us to get or we'd get ourselves killed, so we ran fast as we could back to the house. You don't know how near you came to being motherless."

Mary burst into sobs. Sarah put her arm around her friend. She was sure the stiff plaster didn't offer much comfort. Ma looked away, her face warped with disgust. McCoombs didn't cry nearly so easily. They sat in the darkness and listened to Mary's sobs and the pop pop retort of the guns. Lijah whined about missing the excitement. Daisy just whined. In ten minutes, the only sound was Mrs. Snyder's wheezy breathing.

"Might as well sit here a bit more," Mrs. Snyder said.

"Don't expect it's safe to go back out." She pulled her handkerchief from the bosom of her dress and mopped her brow.

Ma held up her hand. She tilted her head as if listening to a very faint sound. "It ain't over. Listen."

Sarah heard a drum tattoo, tramping feet, shouted commands. She and Lijah followed Ma to the window and fought for the space to peer through the sliver of glass Ma exposed when she carefully drew back the curtain. Union troops ranged all along the east side of the Emmitsburg Road. Hundreds, perhaps thousands of men trampled the McCoombs family fields and those of their neighbors. They were pulling down fences and picking little green peaches off the trees just to throw at each other. Sarah gasped at the destruction.

Ma seemed to have the wrath of God Almighty in her as she bolted out of the house and tramped toward the invaders. She held her fists rigidly against her sides, her chin tucked as if raring for a fight. Sarah scuttled along behind. She didn't know what she could do, encumbered by a plaster cast as she was, but she couldn't let her mother face an entire army alone.

Sarah passed a flag whose letters said 3rd Maine. Near the flag the men's voices sounded different. Sarah had not realized that northerners had such accents. Caissons and cannons and supply wagons crushed the crops. Men drilled in the fields, trampling the wheat. Tents popped up all over the place. Sarah squinted, trying to see if she recognized any of the men near a flag reading 68th Pennsylvania. The 68th Pennsylvania wasn't Micah's unit but perhaps it held some local boys.

The noise and confusion was terrible. "Who are they?" Sarah shouted.

"Men who have no respect for private property," Ma shouted back. It didn't matter to her whether they were a band of truant boys or an entire army; she was determined to drive them off her land. "Now get back to the house."

Sarah dropped back a little, but she didn't turn around. The distance between her and the house was filled with strange men. Better to stay with Ma and risk her wrath than turn around and encounter strangers.

Ma stopped marching when she found a sergeant, the first man they had passed who ranked higher than a private. The sergeant was barking commands at a group of men moving a battery of Parrott guns into position. He seemed determined to ignore her. Ma put her fists on her hips and waited until he swung around. His face glowed red under the mutton chop sideburns. Although he was not as big as Pa, he was a tall man, and strongly built. He towered over Ma. Sarah had the urge to grab Ma's hand and run all the way back to their house, but she dared not say a word lest her mother's fury be loosed on her.

"What?" The sergeant shouted. Ma shook a clenched fist in his face. He took a step back.

"Who is in charge here?" She shouted almost as loudly as the sergeant. "I demand to see the person in charge of this mess."

The sergeant rolled his eyes. He pulled a handkerchief from his chest pocket and rubbed it across his face. He chuckled. "That would be General Sickles, ma'am. I'm sure he'd just love to have a little chit-chat with you right now, wouldn't he, boys?" He pointed toward Abraham Trostle's farm and Ma stormed toward it. Sarah heard the gunners laugh. She smiled sheepishly at the sergeant and hurried after her mother.

Ma marched towards her neighbor's house. Greasy smoke came from the stove pipe. Someone was frying chickens in there. Dozens of horses cropped the grass out front. Ma elbowed her way through the crowd of adjutants and couriers. She climbed two porch steps before an aide stepped into her path. Sarah could tell by the single braid on his sleeve that he was a first lieutenant. His new, polished boots and the cleanliness of his uniform impressed her. He smiled at her, his hand brushing down the hairs of a trim mustache and she wondered if he even noticed how thick and stiff her torso was. Perhaps he was just too much a gentleman to notice such things.

Ma glared at the man. "I've come to see General Sickles."

There was a whispering and rustle among the men before the one who had stepped forward spoke. "General Sickles is rather occupied with battle plans right now, Madame. I am Sheldon Freeborne, one of his aides de camp. May I be of service?" He doffed his hat, and ran a hand over hair as glossy and black as a horse's mane.

"I must talk to the General." Ma swept her arm out, encompassing the whole, chaotic scene. "I want these men out of my meadow. They're crushing the pasture grass."

The lieutenant smiled in a way that made Sarah sure he sympathized with them. She liked him, even his harsh accent. "I assure you, Madame, General Sickles would not have chosen to encamp in your pasture had he any other choice. But the general deemed this position crucial for holding back the enemy."

Ma snorted. "You should be back in Gettysburg, defending the town. That's what the enemy wants: the town. Not these outlying farms."

The sympathetic smile left Lieutenant Freeborne's face. He pointed west towards Seminary Ridge, where Sarah had seen movement and the glint of metal. "The enemy is behind that ridge. They will come this way, attempting to outflank the Union Army. It is imperative we repel them. We will do it here. There will be heavy fighting. I suggest you take your family and flee before it starts, Madam."

"I ain't leaving my land to marauding soldiers, blue or gray," Ma said.

"Then God protect you," the lieutenant said. "You might help Him out a bit, by going into your cellar. Take your poultry with you. While we forbid foraging, some of our boys are quick to liberate a chicken from its coop when the officers are not watching. I dare say the rebels, should we fail in turning them back, will do far worse."

Ma snorted. She tried to take another step up the stairs but men closed rank about the lieutenant, blocking her way. She glared up at them, her hands on her hips. Several of the men turned their eyes aside. They shifted from foot to foot. Ma was a strong presence for being so tiny.

"You ain't going to let me see him, are you?" she said.

"No madam, I am not." The lieutenant stuck out his chin. Sarah imagined he would look no less heroic under fire.

"Then you tell General Sickles that the house he has chosen as his headquarters belongs to a hardworking man who has nine children to support. If he damages anything, it will be like taking food from their mouths. Tell him I expect the farm to be the same when he leaves it as when he came. Better, if there are any gentlemen among you."

"We shall endeavor to stack some firewood," Lieutenant Freeborne said. The answer must have satisfied Ma, for she backed down the stairs and marched home with Sarah running along in her wake, wondering how Ma could get those short little legs of hers to move so fast. They passed the gun emplacement. Several gunners asked Ma if she had seen the General. Ma did not stop to answer.

CHAPTER FIVE
IN THE BELLY OF THE WHALE

Ma surprised Sarah by taking the lieutenant's advice. As soon as she was home, she threw open the cellar doors that leaned into the yard. Days of rain had left about three inches of water sloshing over the hard-packed dirt floor. The bottom step was just above the high water line. Ma turned to Sarah, who stood at the top of the stairs, a chicken cradled in each arm. "This don't look good. You an' Mary an' your brother need to run to Pa's carpentry shed. Get some logs. Big, straight ones: the ones he was going to turn for chair legs. We can lay a false floor of planks on top of 'em to keep us out of the water. Meanwhile, me and Ms. Snyder'll bring down the foodstuffs and settle in the chickens."

Mrs. Snyder peered around Sarah. Her breath whistled in Sarah's ear. "Maybe Mary and I should just go home."

"Ain't no one stopping you," Ma answered. Sarah grimaced. She should have realized that the two women had been neighbors long enough to understand each other, even if they were very different. The Snyders were still there when the floor was laid, the food stacked up, the chickens roosting along the upper shelf. Sarah helped her mother bring down five kitchen chairs, a small table from the parlor, the mantel clock, and the kerosene lantern.

"All set," Ma said. "Hope we don't ever have to use it."

But Ma's hope wasn't to be. It was not much later that Sarah hovered by her bedroom window, watching the ruckus below. It took her a few moments to realize that the thunder was not coming from the dark clouds on the horizon, but from the line of Parrott guns in her field. The guns leaped back as if startled by what they had just done. A cloud of blue gray smoke puffed from their muzzles. A split second later thunder rolled, deep and ominous.

Sarah hustled outside. She clambered down the cellar stairs. The Snyders and her brother were already there. Sarah looked at the mantel clock. It read four. Ma pulled the cellar doors shut and came down last. She held an axe.

"You got that axe to kill rebels, Ma?" Lijah's voice squeaked with excitement. He hopped from foot to foot, unnerving the chickens and making the boards of the makeshift floor bounce.

Ma snorted. "You know your Pa always brings down an axe. We may need it to chop our way out should the house come down over our heads. 'Cepting it's man-made, not God made, this storm ain't no different than any other." She settled onto a stair and laid the axe across her legs.

"Where is Pa?" Lijah asked the question he'd been repeating for over a week.

"Your Pa's way east of here, where it's safe," Ma said. "He's fine, else we'd have heard. Now sit." She thrust a finger at one of the empty chairs.

Not hearing seemed small comfort to Sarah. She settled herself onto a flour barrel where she could swing her feet. She looked around at the half empty barrel of sugar, the barrels of potatoes and apples, the bag of green coffee, and the crocks of sauerkraut that Ma so loved. Hams and dusty herb bunches hung from the rafters. At least they wouldn't starve.

Glass canning jars glimmered in the light of the kerosene lanterns. Sarah counted the jars that had food in them. There weren't many: peas and cherries, mostly. The family had eaten most of last summer's bounty, and little of this summer's crops had yet to produce. She hoped the soldiers didn't tramp down the fields too much. She wished they weren't picking the green peaches. There were an awful lot of empty jars in Ma's cellar needing to be filled before winter came.

"They better not smash down the wheat any more than they have to. It's near to harvestin'," Ma said, mirroring Sarah's thoughts.

Daisy whined and put her chin in Sarah's lap. The thunder of the big guns continued, setting the canning jars to rattling on the shelves like nervous teeth. The rifles sounded like rain on a tin roof. Sometimes the battle ranged near and Sarah could make out the individual pops and men's shouts. Sometimes the noise receded into the background, sounding like a waterfall or the roar of a creek after rain. The shrieking, whistling, moaning of shells before they burst was the most unnerving sound of all, for to Sarah it sounded like lost souls passing overhead. It made her shiver inside her plaster cast.

"If you listen good, you can tell which side is doing the firing," Mrs. Snyder said. She tilted her head to the side like Daisy did when she listened. "That's ours. That's ours. That's their's. That's ours. That's their's."

"How can you tell?" Lijah asked, his voice squeaky with excitement.

Mrs. Snyder wiped her face with her handkerchief. "You remember where our boys were lined up? Remember where they said the Rebs were? Just listen. You can tell which direction things're coming from."

Sarah cocked her head, imitating Mrs. Snyder. She learned to distinguish the deep-toned growl of a gun, the shriek of the shell flying overhead, the sharp crack of the explosion. Soon she could tell which direction they were coming from. She listened, enrapt by the calls and responses of the cannonade. Every time the Union forces did not answer a Confederate gun quickly, her heart sunk, fearing that the enemy had won.

Lijah hopped over to the box of sand where the last few shriveled carrots were stored. He pulled two out and began drumming on the potato barrel. The carrots were old and rubbery and didn't help Lijah keep time very well. The clatter he set up sounded like a box of books falling down a stairway.

"Hush up," Ma snapped. "That sound's driving me batty." To Sarah it was far better than the noise outside, but she understood Ma's nerves being frayed. Besides, Ma could control Lijah's noise and she couldn't control the cannons and the rifles.

"It's the breakfast call: the one called Peas Upon a Trencher," Lijah replied. "Can you tell? Soon's this battle's over I'm going to go up an' get me enlisted as a drummer boy. Then I'll go find Micah and I'll drum for his regiment."

Micah's letters home were always cheery and filled with amusing incidents of camp life. He had never mentioned how horrible battles sounded. Had Micah heard the earth tremble and groan as the shells hit? Sarah hoped he hadn't. Micah's last letter came from a town in Mississippi called Vicksburg that Sarah had never even heard of. But that letter was dated late May. He could be anywhere by now. Did he know what was happening here in his own hometown?

"I said, 'hush up'," Ma said.

"Can't, Ma. I gotta practice so's I can join up." Lijah stuck his tongue out the side of his mouth and pounded all the harder with his rubbery carrots.

"How many drum calls are there, anyway?" Mrs. Snyder asked.

"Lots!" Lijah set down his carrots and began ticking the different calls off on his fingers. "There's drummer's call, what the lead drummer plays to assemble the other musicians first thing in the morning. Then there's reveille, breakfast call, surgeon's call, drill call, assembly of the guard, Adjutant's call, 3 cheers, dinner call, to the color, tattoo, and taps. An' that's just the reg'lar calls. Then there's the marches and the break camps and the battle calls like commence firing and cease firing. A drummer boy's gotta know a lot to direct the troops." He tucked his head and commenced beating the carrots silly.

"I say let him practice," Mrs. Snyder said, "Keeps him busy. But I wouldn't let the boy join up 'til he can play 'em all good enough that his own mother can distinguish one from another."

"That'd take years!" Lijah protested. Mrs. Snyder just smiled.

A strange sound set Sarah's scalp to tingling. It sounded like one of Lijah's Indian war whoops combined with the howl of a wolf and it was so ferocious, so defiant, that Sarah wanted to cower behind a barrel.

"The rebel yell," Ms. Snyder wheezed. "I've heard tell of it."

Feet pounded the wooden floors overhead, then glass broke and the sound of firing rifles came from above. Soldiers were shooting from inside the house. Sarah twitched as someone screamed and something heavy hit the floor, showering her with dust from the rafters overhead.

Lijah dropped his carrot drumsticks. He clambered into Ma's lap, like he used to back when he was a little child. His head was almost as high as Ma's and his feet dangled way down her shins. Sarah hadn't noticed how very tall her brother had grown. With a jolt of panic, she realized that if he went to join up, none of the officers would turn him back.

Ma quoted scripture in the clear, firm voice of authority. "Yea, though I walk through the valley of the shadow of death, I will fear no evil: for thou art with me."

Even within her plaster cast, Sarah felt her spine straighten with the strength of the words. She held her head a little higher, determined not to be afraid.

Lijah's face, wet with tears, shined in the kerosene light. "Is He here, Ma? God is in the valley of the shadow of death, but is He here in the cellar?"

"Jonah was in the belly of the whale three days," Ma answered, "with the mighty ocean roaring over and around him just like this battle's roaring over us. And God was with him and heard his cry." She closed her eyes and began quoting scripture, "Then Jonah prayed unto the Lord his God out of the fish's belly. And said, I cried by reason of mine affliction unto the Lord, and he heard me; out of the belly of hell cried I, and thou heardest my voice. For thou hadst cast me into the deep, in the midst of the sea; and the floods compassed me about: all thy billows and thy waves passed over me.

"Then I said, I am cast out of thy sight; yet I will look again toward thy holy temple. The water compassed me about, even to the soul: the depth closed me round about, the weeds were wrapped about my head. I went down to the bottoms of the mountains; the earth with her bars was about me for ever: yet has thou brought up my life from corruption, O Lord my God."

She went on, as if she could see the page in her mind's eye, and all the time Ma spoke, Sarah wasn't aware of the guns and cannons booming overhead. "When my soul fainted within me I remembered the Lord: and my prayer came in unto thee, into thine holy temple. They that observe lying vanities forsake their own mercy. But I will sacrifice unto thee with the voice of thanksgiving: I will pay that which I have vowed. Salvation is of the Lord."

Ma sat still and calm on the cellar stairs, her eyes closed and her youngest son draped in her lap like a statue of the pieta. She carried the Bible within her, like a backbone to her soul. It strengthened her resolve and gave her purpose. No wonder her mother appeared so strong in spite of her size, Sarah thought.

"What did this Jonah do to deserve getting swallowed up by a whale?" Lijah asked.

"You should know. How many times I told you this story afore?" Ma cuffed the side of Lijah's head gently.

"Lots. But I want to hear you tell it agin," Lijah said.

"Jonah disobeyed God. He refused to do what God had told him to do."

"Did we disobey God? Is that why there's men shooting guns in our house?"

Ma smoothed down Lijah's hair. "The abolitionists think the whole country did, son. They think this war is on account of us allowing the south to keep slaves. But that's something to ask your Pa about when he comes back. I never much studied politics."

"Tell me again what happened to Jonah?" Lijah asked with a big smile. He knew what was coming next.

"Once he'd learned his lesson, the fish swum up to the shore and vomited Jonah right out on the sand."

Lijah sat up tall, his neck straining, stringy as a turtle's neck. "Vomited? Yuck!"

Ma threw back her head and laughed, the first happy sound Sarah had heard in quite a while. It gave her hope that everything was going to turn out all right after all. "What I know is Jonah came out, and he was stronger for it. We will come out all right, too," Ma said, and Sarah was sure that she was right.

CHAPTER SIX
THE SHADOW OF DEATH

It was long past dusk when Ma decided it had been quiet long enough and they could go up the stairs and into the yard. She stood up and stretched, complaining about how tired and stiff her back got when she sat still for so long, then led them up the stairs and into the dark yard. There were no stars in the sky. The gun smoke obscured them. Sarah wondered if the smell of vomit was a memory of Ma's story about the whale. The acrid sting of gunpowder and salt peter drifted across the yard. It mixed with the smells of burned flesh and of salty blood. Sarah could almost taste it. It turned her stomach and made her want to add her own vomit. Groans and cries rose like specters from the darkness. Rifles popped in the east, where Plum Run dipped into the vale behind George Weikert's farm. Lijah often scampered among the boulders there, pretending he was a pirate or an outlaw. Now it was a battlefield.

"This warn't how the summer was supposed to go," Ma muttered. She held the lantern high, revealing vague shapes littering the dark fields like monstrous hail after a storm. Teams of men moved among the mounds. They stooped down, holding their lanterns close. One team picked up a bundle and placed it on a stretcher. It groaned as they passed on their way toward the barn and Sarah realized it was a man. She shuddered. The bundles and mounds were horses and men, some wounded, some dead.

"Lawd almighty! What's you folks doing hea?"

Ma spun toward the voice. Her lantern light spilled onto the porch, revealing a man in a blood-smeared uniform and a wide brimmed felt hat pushed so far back on his head that the brim wreathed his face like a halo. She could tell by the two V's on his sleeve that he was a corporal. Sarah felt a flutter of relief. Here was someone who could help her sort out the ugliness around her.

The flutter died. The dim light had confused her. This man would not help. He, like the people in the well-lit parlor behind him, wore butternut and gray. The farm had fallen into enemy hands.

"This is my farm," Ma said. Her voice came out weak and thin, not at all like the strong voice with which she had demanded to see the man in charge of Union troops earlier that afternoon. She turned, surveying her fields. Sarah caught her stricken look.

The man pulled his hat off and held it to his chest like a real gentleman. "Well, now. I's sorry, ma'am, at the mess we've gone and made in y'all's yard an' house. We went and borrowed a bit of your kitchen supplies, too, but we'll pay y'all back, in good Confederate scrip. We pays for what we takes. It's a bit more pleasant inside, ma'am. Won't y'all come in? We all'll vacate the bedrooms for y'all."

"Not me. I'm going to the barn to check on the animals," Lijah said.

The corporal stepped off the porch. He placed his hand lightly on Lijah's shoulder and bent down so that he was face to face with the boy. It was a gesture Pa often made, and the gentleness of it brought a lump to Sarah's throat. "Ah wouldn't be doing that, son. We's using your barn for surgery and it's none too nice in there. Y'all won't like what you see." Lijah shrugged off the man's hand and hurried toward the bright yellow light shining through the barn door. The man lifted a hand, as if to stop Lijah, but then he let it drop. He watched Lijah go before he took Ma by the elbow and gently led her into the house.

"I'll go in, but do not expect me to do anything that would appear to aid and abet the enemy," Mary said under her breath as she and her ma followed. Sarah gave a sharp, determined nod and took the rear.

The man was wrong. He had said that it was more pleasant inside than out. Sarah found nothing pleasant within. Groans rose up like vapor: weak cries for water, for mother, for help. Wounded confederates lay on the parlor rugs and on the settee. Sarah noted they were using her school books as pillows, and some were streaked with blood. There was blood on the carpets and a large splatter of blood on one wall opposite a broken window. A few men passed among the wounded checking wounds and changing dressings, but they seemed disorganized, confused by the immensity of the suffering around them. A man with his entire head, face and all, wrapped in bloody bandages sat in Pa's big chair, impatiently drumming his fingers on the armrest the way Pa did when Lijah took too long in fetching a book. It struck Sarah as absurd, a point of hilarity amid the horror. She let out a nervous giggle, then shook her head, trying to dispel the bad dream that surrounded her.

But this eerie, surreal scene was no dream.

Sarah felt someone's fingers close around her ankle. She looked down at a barefoot boy, a mere waif of a lad not much older than she. Hair the color of dirty straw hung into his begrimed face. His blue eyes glistened brilliantly, wildly, in a way that made Sarah question his sanity. She looked him over, checked his pants, his tattered shirt, as raggedy as any she'd ever seen on a runaway slave. She saw no wound on him, no smear of blood, yet he seemed to her to be wounded someplace she could not see. He crawled backward, crablike, until he was flat against the wall, then drew his legs up until his chin rested on his knees and began shaking violently, as if chilled to the bone.

"Please, Mother," he said in a voice so plaintive Sarah felt her heart heave within her chest, "Ah'm so very hungry. Has you any bread?"

Ma's voice came from behind Sarah. It was stronger now, as if Ma had gotten over some of her shock and was ready to take command again. "Sarah, go back and get our bread from the cellar. Hand it round while me and Mrs. Snyder stir up another batch."

"Mary can take the water pitcher and dipper around for these men." Mrs. Snyder's voice sounded as steely as Ma's.

"But, Mother," Mary protested. "They're confederates! Don't make me go among them."

"They're boys," Mrs. Snyder answered, "and they're hungry and scared and far from home. So we will feed them and bind their wounds. I pray some woman does the same for Jacob or Martin, if'n it comes to that."

"And for my Micah down in Tennessee," Ma added.

Sarah found handing out chunks of bread slathered in Ma's cherry jam a more difficult task than she had imagined. The cast stopped her from bending to reach the men on the floor. Many were just as incapable of reaching up to her. She had just learned to precariously balance herself as she leaned from the hips, her legs splayed out for balance, when Lijah came back.

His face was red and puffy. Streaks of mud showed where he had brushed away tears. He held his shoulders tight up against his ears, his hands in white knuckled fists. "They shot Beatrice. I'm going to kill a confederate! I hate them! I hate you all."

Sarah tried to hush him. The papers had been filled with stories of rebel atrocities. Who knew what these men could do if provoked. She sucked in her breath, waiting for retribution. None of the wounded or their attendants said a word. The gentlemanly corporal from the front porch came up behind Lijah and laid a hand on his shoulder. "I'd hate us, too, son, if'n I was you," he said.

Lijah squirmed out from under the corporal's hand. "I'm not your son!" he shouted, his fists curling and uncurling at the end of his tensed arms. He stomped upstairs to his bedroom and slammed the door. In a moment Sarah heard Lijah's disorganized drumming. His anger made him no better than he had been when he practiced with two carrots in the cellar.

"I'm sorry, sir. He's just a boy, and you've killed the old, broken down horse he loved so much," Sarah said.

The man waved his hand, dismissing her concerns. "I know. I got me a boy 'bout his age back in Huntsville. My Emmit would take no more kindly to someone killing his pet goat than your brother did his horse. But you know, Miss, not that I'm making excuses, but we may not have killed y'all's Beatrice. There was heavy fighting here. Both sides used a mighty lot 'o lead." He sighed and fluffed up a parlor pillow under the head of a one-legged man who was moaning, unconscious, on the floor. When he straightened, he had a smile on his face. He hooked his thumb over his shoulder.

"I couldn't help but notice y'alls piano there. We'd be mighty obliged if you played for us. It'd take these fellow's minds off their hurts."

Mary stood up stiffly and cleared her throat. "The piano is mine. I regret, Sir, that I only know songs which would comfort a union solider."

"Any song would be a comfort, miss. Please." The corporal asked so gently that Sarah was tempted to sit at the piano and play for him. Her playing would be no comfort. Sarah played piano nearly as badly as her brother drummed. But as Mrs. Snyder had said, these men were hungry, and hurt, and far from home. Surely playing the piano for them could not be considered aiding and abetting the enemy. She would do it. For Micah's sake. She gave Mary a plaintive look.

Mary rolled her eyes in protest, but she sat on the bench and sorted through her music. She banged out a defiant Columbia, Gem of the Ocean, her shoulders as stiff and squared as any soldier on review, then continued with a rousing Yankee Doodle, followed by Rally 'Round the Flag and The Battle Hymn of the Republic. When she got to the chorus of Union Forever, Sarah joined in. A union of rivers and a union of lakes, A union of land and a union of States, A union of hearts and a union of hands, And the flag of our union forever. The cast made it hard for her to suck in enough air, so her voice came out embarrassingly thin and wheezy.

Sarah couldn't remember any more of the words than when she'd sung to Buford's troops, but the soldiers didn't seem to mind any more than the Union Cavalry had. Those who could sit up did so, leaning on their elbows. The windows filled with the faces of healthy, unwounded men who were camping in the yard outside. It was enough to make Sarah's heart break within her stony cast. Mary, staring at her music instead of her audience, seemed unaffected. She turned and glared defiantly, her eyes squinted down in a meanness of spirit.

The Corporal sighed and wiped away a tear. It surprised Sarah. She thought her Pa the only grown man with a tender heart. "My wife's name is Mary, same as you. And same as you, she plays real nice. We had us a piano, 'fore the Union army passed through."

Mary's shoulders seemed to lose their starch. "A Union solider destroyed your piano?"

"Yes'm."

Mary threw herself protectively over the piano, guarding it with her body.

"I ain't the type to hold no grudge." He held his hat between his hands again as he gave Mary a humble, low bow. "Things like that's what happens in war. I ain't going to harm your piano none. Boys, let's give back some. Let's sing for the girls."

The men outside sang in deep, strong voices. Inside, those that could, sang. Those who could not sing clapped or beat time. The man who sat in Pa's big chair with his head bandaged continued to drum his fingers. Some could not even do that.

They began with a mournful rendition of Dixie. Then came All Quiet Along the Potomac and The Vacant Chair, both sung so plaintively that Mary's heart softened. She turned back to the piano and played Just Before the Battle, Mother and The Girl I Left Behind Me, and Tenting on the Old Camp Ground before Ma and Mrs. Snyder brought out more bread and jam. Sarah and Mary carried around the water pitcher one more time while their mothers used the bandages they had made while sitting in the porch rockers, and then they climbed the stairs to the bedrooms the soldiers had vacated for them.

Lijah lay fully dressed in the middle of the bed, his arms thrown out as if to embrace the world. His face, though smeared with tear streaks, had no traces of anger left. Sarah knew he would heal. Without waking him, Sarah pulled off his overalls and draped them over the footboard. She bent to tenderly kiss her brother's forehead where his hair fanned out like a sheaf of ripened wheat. Sarah's thighs felt bruised were where her cast pressed against them. She knew that she, too, would heal.

She wasn't so sure about the blond waif cowering in the corner of the parlor or the man drumming his fingers on the arm of Pa's chair.

Sarah lay on her bed, as helpless as a turtle within her rigid cast. A cricket chorus rose up as if denying that anything terrible had happened on that long, hot July day. How did the stars manage to keep moving in their courses, the crickets to sing amidst so much sadness and brokenness?

Though her body was exhausted, Sarah's mind darted wildly through images of the horrible suffering she had witnessed. She stared at the ceiling and wondered if she would ever be able to sleep again. The next thing she wondered was why the sky was bright and the birds were singing, and she found that she had slept in spite of it all.

CHAPTER SEVEN
THE SHIFTING WIND

"Morning!" Lijah leapt out of bed. He looked as fresh as the birds that twittered outside, ready to face the day with the renewed vigor of a good night's sleep.

"He's so cheery," Mary said as he bounded out the door. "It's as if he doesn't even remember what happened yesterday."

"I don't think he does," Sarah answered, her heart grieving. He was halfway down the stairs when the patter of his feet slowed, then stopped. A moment later he was back in the bedroom.

"There's soldiers everywhere, and they saw me in my under drawers." He snatched his overalls off the foot board and stepped into them. "Why didn't someone tell me my pants weren't hanging on their peg by the back door?"

"Didn't have a chance, bright eyes. You were just too quick for us." Sarah tried to sound cheerful, to give her brother the spirit he needed to continue. It wasn't easy. Mary pushed Sarah out of bed and pulled her dress over her head.

"I ain't going down," Lijah crossed his arms over his chest, daring them to make him. "I ain't going to face those men."

"That might be for the best," Mary said. "No sense starting a battle in your own parlor. I'll bring you breakfast."

Ma was flipping pancakes at the stove when Sarah walked in. She glanced up for just a moment, but it was long enough for Sarah to see the dark rings beneath her mother's eyes and wonder whether she had rested at all last night. Mrs. Snyder, who had probably worked more in the past week than in the past year, looked even more tired and disheveled. She was throwing her considerable weight into mixing up another batch of batter, but she stabbed her finger toward a plate of steaming pancakes. Sarah took them to distribute among the men.

At first Sarah's conscience balked at the primitiveness of handing a pancake to a man without offering him a plate or fork, but she soon realized that the McCoombs household didn't own enough plates and forks to feed such a multitude. And the men didn't seem to mind. They seemed truly grateful with the humble fare.

Sarah found the Corporal bending over one of his wounded men in the parlor. He tenderly probed the man's stomach the same way Ma did when one of her children had a stomach ache, but Sarah knew he was looking for minie balls. Sarah's stomach lurched, as if a cold, dead hunk of lead lay at its depths.

The Corporal looked up with eyes as tired as her mother's. He offered her a warm smile and she offered him a pancake.

He rolled it into a log before taking a bite. "Thank ye kindly. How's y'alls brother doing this morn?"

"He's still rather surly."

She looked around, taking account. Some of the men who had been there the night before were gone. Some, she was sure, had not lasted the night. But the absence of others surprised her. "That blond boy: the one who was sitting in the corner. Where is he?"

The Corporal sighed. He placed his hands on his thighs and pushed himself to a stand. "Well, Miss, Private Gemmy Smith took a French furlough."

"What's a French furlough?" Sarah asked.

"Means he went absent without leave. Probably half way home to Alabama by now."

Sarah gasped. "He deserted?"

"Desertion's a hard word, with harsh consequences." He peered out the window, as if looking for the boy along the Emmitsville Road. "I hope he makes it."

"What happens if he doesn't? If he gets caught?" Sarah handed her last pancake to a one-legged man who held it against his chest as if it were made of gold.

"If'n it's by your side, he'll spend the rest of the war in a prison camp. If'n it's by our side he'll be shot. Lessen he comes back on his own," the Corporal said.

"But the poor thing wasn't in his right mind!" Sarah said.

The Corporal looked at her. "You think anyone engaged in war is? We's all a little crazy or we couldn't be shooting' at each other, now could we? If'n anything, the boy finally figured out how insane this all was, so he up and skedaddled. But ah don't think being in y'alls right mind is a qualification for getting' into the army, and it sure ain't no excuse to get out."

He took the empty plate from her hand and pressed a piece of paper and a stubby pencil into them. "I'll git us some more pancakes if'n you'd go around the room and collect names and hometowns from these here boys, so's you can write to their folks if'n it's needed. These boys is in need of some female tenderness."

Sarah glanced at men lying on blood soaked carpets, draped over the settee, sprawled in the hall. Panic made her heart thump against her cast. These men had lived through horrors too terrible to describe. Her mind scrambled to find the words to write, but there were none. How could she commit any of that to paper? How could she subject their families to it? She could not, would not write letters for these men. It was too cruel.

Sarah cast about for something else to do. "Surely there is something else we should be doing: something more medical than handing out pancakes and taking down addresses?"

The Corporal shrugged. "If'n there is, Miss, we'd need a medical man to tell us, an' they was in the barn a' fore they moved on to another site an' left us to fend for ourselves. I ain't no trained orderly, even, to know what I's supposed to do. I'm just a fighting man."

She shot him a look of shock. "If you're not trained to treat the wounded, why are you here instead of with your unit?"

"'Cause there ain't enough men in my unit to make it worth putting in to fight. They's all dead or wounded." A look someplace between guilt and regret clouded his face. He ducked through the doorway before Sarah could ask any more questions.

Sarah made the rounds, placing the paper on her own plaster-casted stomach and writing upside down. Men told her names of fallen comrades and the circumstances under which they fell. They begged her to write comforting words, both to their own relatives and those of the deceased. Sarah could not promise she would. She did not know what to say. She came to the man who sat in Pa's chair. His fingers drummed the chair arm, just as they had last night. She wondered if he could answer her through his bandages.

"Excuse me." Sarah laid a hand on his shoulder. The man did not pause. She tapped his shoulder. His fingers continued drumming the arm of the chair.

"He doesn't seem to hear me," she said to the Corporal, who reentered the room with another plate of pancakes.

"Don't think he do," the Corporal answered. "Leastways, don't think he got enough reasoning left to know what to make of speech, even if he hears it. This'n wandered in over the fields. The top half of his head had a hole in it big enough to stick my fist in. He ain't from our outfit, but we bandaged him up and hope someone comes looking for him."

The Corporal let out a sigh that sounded like he released all the misery a man could possibly hold. "I 'spect he'll starve to death afore long. At least he don't appear to be feeling no pain. Some of these others would give up their minds to be free from pain."

He snapped his fingers and brightened a little. "That reminds me: y'all ain't got nothing red we kin hang outside? Any bit a cloth will do. It'd be real nice if we had another piece for the barn as well."

Sarah must have looked puzzled. The Corporal explained that red let the enemy know that the building was a makeshift hospital and should therefore not be fired upon. It would not guarantee their safety, not like a real yellow hospital flag, the kind with the green H emblazoned on it, but there weren't enough real hospital flags to go around, so both sides had resorted to using red scraps to mark hospitals.

Sarah felt herself sway. "You mean it's not over?"

"It ain't even close to being over," the Corporal answered. "We expect another battle soon. Scuttlebutt is that it'll be a big one. General Lee ain't one to leave a fight undecided if'n he can help it." Sarah directed him back to the kitchen to ask her mother. In half an hour a pair of Pa's long johns fluttered from the barn roof. Another pair adorned the weathervane on the house. Sarah protested that underwear had no place being exhibited like that, but Ma argued that they were the biggest pieces of red cloth the family owned. If a red flag was going to be the only thing that stood between her family and a shelling, she wanted the largest flag possible.

Sarah didn't even wonder if it was thunder when the early afternoon cannonade began. The very foundations of the house trembled. Speech, even shouting, was futile against the cannon's roar. The Corporal took the bandages from Sarah and pointed toward the cellar door. Sarah collected Lijah and they scurried down while the cannons in her yard and along Seminary Ridge hurled death east toward the Union Army hidden behind Cemetery Ridge. Within minutes, the Union cannons answered.

"Makes yesterday sound like a practice shoot, don't it?" Mrs. Snyder shouted above the din. No one answered her. Sarah squeezed her eyes shut. She pressed her open palms to her ears. The cannon's roar could not drown out the scream of wounded horses, the frenzied shouts of men or the dark memory of shapes strewn across her yard. She had thought nothing could be worse than yesterday's carnage.

Artillery pounded the earth senseless for two full hours. When it suddenly stopped, the silence roared in Sarah's ears even louder than the cannons had. She opened her eyes and looked at the others. Mary hunched in her chair, her shiny wet face cradled in trembling hands. Next to her, her mother slept sprawled in her chair, her face tilted toward the ceiling, her mouth gaping open, her hands hanging limp at her sides.

Sarah averted her eyes. She had seen the dead look just as still, just as peaceful.

Lijah huddled on his mother's lap. His face looked stricken, silent, and white, the anger pounded out of him by the relentless battle. Ma's face exhibited confusion and powerlessness, both surprising in the dominant little woman. Sarah felt separated from them, as if she were looking at a photograph of people she didn't know, who were sitting in a room she had never visited.

Mrs. Snyder woke with a snort. She smacked her lips and glanced around with bleary eyes. "The cannonade is over," she said, stating the obvious. She began to stand but halted halfway up. The eerie howl of the rebel yell, thin and high as ghostly memories of boys at play, weak as it drifted over great distance, made the hair on Sarah's head stand on end. The yell lingered, was met by the deep, chesty Union shout, then both sounds drowned in the patter and pop of rifles, clattering like the Snyder's wagon as it careened down the road. Lijah buried his face in his mother's stomach. Sarah closed her eyes again and pressed her palms so tightly over her ears that her eardrums felt the pressure. Her hearing filled with the sound of her own blood coursing through her. In mere minutes it was quiet again. Soon the Corporal knocked an all-clear on the cellar door.

Sarah noted a strange change as she attended the wounded that afternoon. The breeze had died, leaving the farm in a pocket of still, stifling air. The mood of the men was just as stifling. A somber pall hung over them, a sullenness that seemed to add to their pain and suck them into their own silent thoughts. There were no songs that evening. Whispers and rumors rippled through the men. One by one, soldiers bivouacked outside melted into the darkness.

The Corporal helped move some of the wounded into wagons, explaining vaguely that they were bound for a more permanent hospital. Before Sarah had a chance to say goodbye, he, too disappeared into the night. She listened to the creak of harness. The rumbling of wheels faded into the distance before she turned to the men who were left, the men with severe belly or chest wounds or who were unconscious. None were able to eat. Sarah knew they had been left to die. She and the other three women cleaned wounds and offered water, but there was not much to do.

Mrs. Snyder, then Mary, and finally Ma drifted upstairs to bed until Sarah alone stood in the silent darkness.

She stepped out onto the porch, picking her way carefully among the men who lay there. The wind shifted, driving low clouds scuttling across the moon and veiling the farm in comforting darkness, hiding the carnage from her eyes. Fat raindrops cleared gun smoke and the sour smell of death from the air. The breeze felt cool and fresh on her face. Yellow lantern light bobbed and swayed in the distance. It must be hard for the lantern bearers to look for wounded among the dead in the rain.

Sarah leaned against the porch pillar. Dawn was only a few hours away. She wondered if the new day would bring more horror or relief. She felt nothing. She was too tired to feel. As she rested there, a sound rose up on the north end of Cemetery Ridge, where the Union Line was. It was a deep cheer, from the bellies of what must have been a thousand men. Sarah stood erect. The sound rolled toward her, southward along Cemetery Ridge, gaining intensity and joy as it went. It reached the bottom of the Ridge at Big Round Top, then echoed back, building strength until the whole valley filled with its reverberations. She shivered, but it was not from cold. A wounded man stirred near her feet, his eyes glistening in the faint, passing moonlight.

"Damn," he muttered through parched lips. "We've lost."

"I am sorry," she said, and to her own amazement found that what she had said was true. Unable to bend, Sarah stroked the man's arm with her foot. She turned to tell the Corporal the news, but remembered he had gone with the wagon. She had never even asked him his name.

CHAPTER EIGHT
GHOSTLY MEMORIES

It was over. The Union army had won. Sarah was too exhausted to care. She had become compressed within her plaster cast like the load within a rifle barrel. She stretched, releasing her back with a series of pops and cracks. The knotted muscles in her forehead and neck eased. She suddenly felt as loose-jointed as the Snyder's wagon, liable to clatter into pieces at any moment. Sarah clutched the doorframe. The stairs to her bedroom seemed insurmountably steep. She dropped into a kitchen chair and tried to rest her body on the table, but the cast stopped her. She pushed the chair back, leaned her cast into her thighs, and fell asleep with her head and forearms on the kitchen table.

"Psst. Sarah, doll, wake up." The voice tried to pull Sarah out of her sleep, but it was a deep and dreamless sleep and it did not want to release her. She groggily rubbed her eyes, too tired to connect one thought with another. A gaunt, disheveled ghost of a Union soldier knelt beside her. She gasped at his closeness and her heart beat a retreat in her ears.

The soldier's hair hung down, black and greasy, into a face so taut that the cheekbones stood out sharply. He smelled of mold and rot and something even less healthy. But the most frightening part of him were his eyes. The man's gaze darted around the kitchen as if following unseen ghosts.

"Gemmy Smith went to Alabama," she said, her foggy mind assuming somewhat crazily that he had come to haunt the haunted boy who had gone on a French furlough.

The soldier tilted his head, exposing one clear, bright steel gray eye. "Don't you recognize me, Sarah doll? It's me. Martin."

Sarah tried to shake the cobwebs from her mind. She must be dreaming. Mary's handsome older brother had grown more handsome and heroic in Sarah's imagination over the months of separation. The apparition before her looked like the hundreds of powder-smeared men who had swirled destructively around her house as part of the terrible human thunderstorm. This could not be Martin. She tried to look him in the eye, but he jerked back as if struck. His eyes rested everywhere but on her.

"Where's my mother? Where's Mary? Where's Hans?" His voice jolted her awake again and she realized that she had drifted off to sleep. She glanced at the gaunt young man and he twitched.

"Martin's in Winchester," she mumbled.

He smiled patiently, placing a trembling hand on her forearm, then pulling it away as if she were red hot. "I was in Winchester. I got captured there. But I escaped. I snuck here through enemy lines. Been hiding out in the woods, waiting for things to die down. Lord almighty, what a fight's been going on here! I got to my house a little while back. It was empty. Where is everybody?"

Sarah tried hard to focus, but sleep threatened to engulf her. "Martin's sister and Ma are upstairs, sleeping," she said. "His brother took the horse and wagon before the battle started. He and his pa are in Winchester."

"No, Sarah doll. Look at me. I'm here. Pa's died of dysentery. I got a case of it myself, but I'll survive. Oh, I give up. You sleep. We'll talk in the morning." He gently settled her back on the table. The last thing she heard was his footsteps mounting the stairs.

Sarah sat up and blinked owlishly. At first she thought it was barely dawn, for the kitchen light was gray. Then she noticed rain, sheeting down beyond the open door as if God himself were crying over the destruction. Mary leaned against the doorsill, looking out into the soggy yard. The two mothers were making pancakes. Although it felt like she had just fallen asleep, Sarah knew she must have slept long and hard.

Sarah had a vague memory of Martin hovering close. But it wasn't Martin; it was an odd mix between her handsome neighbor and the rag tag troops she had nursed the past two days. She must have dreamt it.

Mrs. Snyder looked up from her batter bowl. "My boy Martin's back. We whooped and hollered loud enough to wake the dead and you slept right through it. When he told us about Pa, we wailed so hard you'd think folks in town would've come running. Still you slept. "

"She's worked hard," Ma said gruffly. "Ain't easy dragging all that plaster 'round."

Mrs. Snyder grunted in agreement. "My boy's tired, too. Got a heavy heart, filled to bursting with all the ugliness he's seen. It's no wonder he'd rather be out there keeping busy than sitting in here talking."

"Look at him out there," Mary said.

Sarah dragged herself from her chair and joined her friend. Martin and Lijah were pulling apart abandoned confederate supply crates to repair the chicken coop. They didn't seem to notice the rain dripping off the tips of their noses. Doing something constructive, even something as simple as repairing a coop seemed more important than keeping dry. Martin clutched his stomach and lurched for the outhouse and Sarah remembered what he had said about him and his Pa last night. It helped explain the smell he'd had. It had been no dream: the Martin working on the coop was as bedraggled and gaunt as the Martin who had awoken her last night. The dashing young soldier was no more.

Sarah felt her cheeks flush. She had imagined Martin's homecoming many times as a romantic affair, when he would look at her and appreciate the fine women she'd become. Instead, Martin came home to a girl babbling gibberish. She swallowed back tears of regret for having ruined their reunion. "I'm sorry about your Pa."

"It was providence." Mary shrugged. "I suppose I'll cry later, but not now. Not with Martin back."

Sarah stared at her friend. She wouldn't be so calm if it was her pa who'd died. Then again, her pa wasn't known through the valley for beating his womenfolk during bellowing, drunken fits.

Sarah turned and stumbled blindly up the stairs to her bedroom. She threw herself face first on her bed. So many people's dreams had been shattered: her and Martin's and the crazy boy on a French furlough's, and ten thousand others besides. Martin had marched away in a uniform made of shoddy, a new style of woolen cloth made from pressed woolen fibers. The uniform had disintegrated. So had the man. Both hung slack and lifeless. Sarah thought of the gaunt cheeks and sunken eyes that had confronted her last night. She shuddered. That ghost wasn't her Martin. She wanted no part of a ghostly, twitching Martin with the haunted eyes. And surely he did not want the babbling girl encased in a plaster shell.

When Martin and his mother and sister moved back to their own house, dragging their oilcloth-wrapped piano down the muddy road during a lull in the rain, Sarah did not say goodbye. She could no more find the words to say to him than she had been able to write those letters to the families of dead soldiers.

After they were gone, Sarah trudged down to the kitchen. Ma pulled a hand out of the bread dough and brushed a stray hair from her face, leaving a streak of white across her forehead. Ma had used up close to a month's supply of flour feeding the wounded. She was beginning to look as empty as the flour barrel.

"You didn't give Martin a proper welcome," Ma said.

"The war's changed him." Sarah looked out the window, down the road toward the Snyder farm.

"It's for the best," Ma said. "A strapping young man like Martin Snyder needs a healthy wife to bear him children."

Sarah glared at her mother, hurt by her lack of support. Martin Snyder didn't look so strapping to her. "He's got dysentery."

"He'll be healed of the dysentery. No telling if the cast will heal your back. Now forget your foolishness and concentrate on becoming a teacher."

Ma put a hand to the small of her back and groaned softly. Sarah poured her mother a cup of coffee and gently edged her from the bread bowl. She pushed Ma's words deep into the dough with the heels of her hands. She folded the dough over, burying her grief, then pressed it away from her again and again until the dough was as soft and smooth as a baby's bottom. But kneading dough didn't bury the pain of Ma's words any more than burying the dead overcame the horror of the battle.

Lijah stuck his dripping wet head in the kitchen window. "Hey Ma! There's wagons coming."

Sarah grabbed a towel to wipe the dough from her hands. She followed Lijah and her mother out to meet the parade of wagons and carriages coming south from town. She skirted a body swollen and blackened by the sun. Sarah tried to avert her gaze, but it fell on another, fresher corpse. Raindrops put splashing, pulsing rings in the crimson puddle surrounding it. For a brief, frightening moment, Sarah imagined the puddle pulsing with the dead man's life blood. She pulled the horror down deep into her, suppressing it.

Sarah tilted her head back. The rain felt shockingly cold.

The men who rode their horses at the front of the column pointed towards her neighbor's fields. A carriage pulled over. Its occupants climbed down and walked hunched, as if searching for something amid the rubble and bodies in the battered wheat. The rest of the column continued on.

"Good morning, Ma'am," the man at the front of the column said when he'd ridden up to the McCoombs. "Happy Fourth of July."

Sarah blinked, stunned by the incongruity of a holiday amidst the carnage. The man tipped his oilcloth-covered hat, sending a sheet of water onto his horse's mane. His poncho made it impossible to know if he wore a uniform, but he had an air of authority which convinced Sarah he was a high-ranking officer.

"Won't be much celebrating here," Ma turned to survey her damaged fields.

"Least we can celebrate a victory," the man answered. "Got any wounded at your house?"

"Confederate," Ma spat the word out as if it were some kind of curse. The man conferred with the others in low voices. He turned back to Sarah's mother, pointing over his shoulder at another poncho-clad man on a roan mare.

"We'll use your home as a field hospital, then. The medical corps is already throwing up a real one, so we'll be out of your hair soon. Doctor Cunningham here will stay with you and see to your patients. He's not regular army, but he's good. Gregory," he said, turning in his saddle to shout instructions at another of the men, "detail a company to move those Rebs out of the house and onto the lawn. And send a couple of orderlies to help Cunningham. Tell the searchers they can bring wounded here." He stuck his spurs in his mount before Ma could protest. The column moved on.

Sarah studied the man they left behind. Doctor Cunningham was small and slight boned. He had pale gray eyes, as colorless as the overcast sky. Rain dripped from a bushy mustache that drooped around his mouth like a frown, out of place on his smooth face.

"Sorry to intrude, Ma'am. A person's home should be free from the horrors of war." He tipped his hat, sending down a small shower just as his superior had. His strange accent played on Sarah's memories. She knew she had heard it once before.

"Too late for that now. As long as you're going to help with the wounded I won't mind feeding you," Ma turned and they followed her back through the muddy yard.

Sarah put her hand on the sorrel mare's neck and peered up at the doctor. "You're from Maine, aren't you?"

"Ayup. How'd you know?"

"Some of the artillery men who were here sounded like you."

"There were Maine men here?" The doctor squinted out towards the field as if expecting to see friends.

"Lots of 'em!" Lijah's face brightened with the memory. "An' Pennsylvania. An' New York an' New Hampshire and' Massachusetts and New Jersey! There was tons of 'em! But you ain't regular army, are you?"

Doctor Cunningham laughed, amused by Lijah's impertinence. "I'm not a military man at all. I'm what the army calls a contract surgeon. They hired me because they're shooting more men than they can heal on their own."

"I'm Lijah McCoombs and I'm ten years old. I ain't army yet, but I'm going to join up just as soon as I learn me all the drum tattoos."

The doctor swung off his horse. He looped its reins over the porch rail, then shook Lijah's hand. "That's a noble thing for a ten-year-old boy to aspire to, Elijah McCoombs. But did you know that the U.S. Army could use your help right now?"

"Really?" Lijah leaned in close, his eyes as big as goose eggs.

"Ayup." The doctor squatted so that his head was level with Lijah's. He handed the boy a canteen and pointed toward the fields. "Those men walking around out there are citizens of Gettysburg, just like you, and they are searching for survivors. I learned at Chancelorville that some of the wounded are hard to find. They crawl under bushes and behind rocks, where they think they'll be safe, and they end up bleeding to death before anybody finds them. The thing they need more than anything else is water. Take this canteen. If you find a man alive, give him water and shout until a search party comes. You could be a hero. You could save a life."

Lijah didn't say goodbye. His blond hair streamed back as he ran, his head high, his step full of purpose. He was a boy who had needed a mission and was grateful to have one.

Sarah needed a mission, too.

She followed the doctor as he familiarized himself with his patients and then she led him to the barn and showed him the small barn door that the confederate surgeon had taken off its hinges and used as a table. The pile of arms and legs next to it looked as random as a pile of brush cut from the hedges. She could not take her eyes from it.

Doctor Cunningham put an arm around her shoulders and steered her away. Once they were outside, he rapped on her torso.

"What's this?"

"The doctor says I have scoliosis. And kyphosis, too." Sarah blushed as if she was admitting some horrible sin.

He studied her face seriously, his brows knit together over his eyes in concern. There was neither horror nor condemnation in his eyes. "Does the cast help?"

She would have shrugged if not for the cast. "Can't say. Been on only a couple of weeks."

"What don't kill you will heal you, right?" The corners of his mouth twitched up under the bushy mustache. His eyes sparkled.

"Ma believes in modern medicine. She says what's gotta be, gotta be."

Doctor Cunningham snorted an acknowledgement. He went back to the barn to set up his medical supplies. His orderlies arrived and attended to the broken, mangled men that searchers carried over the fields and lined up by the side of the barn. Sarah nursed newcomers in the parlor and on the porch. She visited her old charges, who now lay in the yard, soaked by the rain and frightened by the change in command. She rigged a tarp for them using her quilt. She helped her mother in the kitchen. It felt good to keep busy. Sarah concentrated on the movements of her hands to shield herself from the ugliness. The hours slid by quickly. There was much to do.

They stopped for lunch, thin chicken gravy over thinner slices of bread. Ma was stretching the last of the flour and chickens. The Doctor grabbed a hasty bite, not even changing out of his blood-splattered surgery apron. But Lijah dallied, mushing together his gravy and bread but not eating it.

Ma jabbed her fork toward his plate. "Eat. You need your strength."

Lijah set his fork down with a sigh. His face looked pinched and worn, as if he had aged twenty years. "They line up the dead," he said, "Union in one row an' Rebs in t'other. Then they dig a long trench and put the bodies in. They write what they can on old boards, like the ones what me and Martin used to mend the chicken coop. They stick the boards up like gravestones. Sometimes the board got a name and hometown on it. Sometimes just a regiment. Some boards just say 'Union' or 'Confed.' Some don't got no boards at all."

"Eat," Ma insisted.

Lijah held one stiff arm out in front of him, his fingers clenched in a claw. "One corpse got stiff with one arm up, like this. Every time they threw dirt on him, the arm popped back up. Finally a man took a shovel and broke it so's they could go on with the burying."

"Lijah!" Ma's voice was filled with horror.

Lijah turned vacant eyes toward Ma. He seemed to be looking through her. "Ain't like it hurt him none, him being dead and all."

Ma pushed herself away from the table. She scraped her son's plate into Daisy's dish. Daisy, who had been cowering under the table, swallowed the soggy bread in great, wolfing bites.

"We need to tie Daisy up," Lijah said, abstractly watching her eat. "Patrols in town're shooting dogs. They's running away with amputated arms and legs. Not that the men need 'em no more."

Ma scraped her own plate into Daisy's bowl. "I'll keep her in, then. She ain't been acting herself anyhow, not since the fighting began. You ain't going outside no more either. You've seen more than a boy need see."

"I gotta," he answered as he scooted back his chair. "Gotta help spread lime, to keep down the smell an' the disease. Gotta help burn horses. Soldiers say dead horses ain't their responsibility and us citizens gotta burn 'em."

Ma grabbed a chairback. She closed her eyes, but Sarah couldn't tell if Ma was praying or trying to keep from fainting away. By the time she opened her eyes, Lijah was gone. "This ain't how it was supposed to be," Ma said. Sarah wanted to know what Ma meant, but she dared not ask. Ma looked so tired, so tiny. Sarah feared her questions might break her.

Evening enshrouded the battlefield in purple velvet light, yet orderlies still brought men from the barn's surgery table to Sarah's care. There were young men and old. They wore both blue and gray. Sarah treated them all with the same compassion. Like Ma had said, they were hungry and scared and far from home. Reb or Yank, they all had mothers somewhere.

She got down on the porch on hands and knees to comfort a young drummer boy who said he had come all the way from Georgia just to lose a leg. His name was Jimmy Harlow. He was about Lijah's age, with the same blue eyes and the same smattering of freckles across his nose. Sarah wondered if Jimmy could talk some sense into Lijah, if he still wanted to go to war after all he had seen.

The last new patient of the evening lay on his stomach on the stretcher, his bare shoulder covered in bandages soaked through with bright red blood. Though his new, polished boots were smeared with horse manure and mud and the trousers of his uniform were tattered, Sarah recognized the gallant aide de camp who had stopped her mother from seeing General Sickles. She struggled down to hands and knees and stroked his hair, still as glossy and black as a horse's mane.

"I lost my hat." First Lieutenant Sheldon Freeborne offered her a weak, sickly smile. He brought up a hand to brush down the hairs of his trim mustache. But there was no hand there: just a bandaged stump at which he stared in disbelief before allowing it to drop to the ground beside him.

"We can find you another hat," Sarah answered. "You are quite a hero."

He winced, as if her words hurt worse than the loss of his hand or the wound in his shoulder. "Not me. My mother said aides de camp were too valuable to put in the front lines. I thought I was safe at the general's headquarters. But we were overrun. I panicked. I turned and I ran. I was a coward, and to prove it, I've been shot in the back." Tears piled up in the corner of his eyes. He turned his face to the ground.

"I am sure many a brave hero has done that," Sarah said as soothingly as she could.

He let out a sigh and turned his face to the side again, peering up at her. "Write to my mother, will you? But lie to her. Tell her I was brave and did my duty. Tell her I died standing tall in the face of the enemy."

"You can tell her yourself, when you get home." A spark of panic ignited in Sarah's stomach. She fought it down. "You won't die. I'll nurse you until you're well enough to travel. Now, go to sleep. You need your rest." Sarah struggled to her feet. It was no easy task with the cast. She'd almost gotten herself upright by hauling on a table leg when Lieutenant Freeborne nearly knocked her down by batting at her with his stump.

"Promise me you will visit me in the morning?" The desperation in his voice made her heart want to break. She promised.

But in the morning he was gone.

CHAPTER NINE
A CURSE UNTO THE GENERATIONS

Sarah wrote. She took out pen and paper and told First Lieutenant Sheldon Freeborne's folks in New York how brave he had been. She wrote words of comfort to families of other soldiers in Massachusetts and Pennsylvania, New Jersey and New Hampshire. She smoothed out the list, which the Corporal from Alabama had urged her make, and wrote to families from Texas and Arkansas, Georgia and South Carolina. She made sure that these letters were just as comforting as those she'd sent to the Northern families.

Her heart full to breaking, Sarah folded the letters with deliberate care and sealed them with flour paste. She addressed them as completely as she could. Some not only bore the names of the dead man's parents but of streets and towns. Others only said "to the parents of" and the name of a state. But unlike the buried bodies, each letter had at least some small bit of identification. Later, when there was time, she would have Lijah run into town and buy stamps. He could use her pin money.

When her hand cramped and words swam before tired eyes, Sarah attended her patients. She tried to ignore the bruises where the cast pressed into her thighs as she offered water, changed bloody compresses, held shaking hands. She talked and fed and comforted, but always returned to her letters. Whenever she thought she had finished, another death made for another letter.

When she became too tired to write and too pained to attend, Sarah leaned against the doorsill and looked down the Emmitsburg road past the cannon-rutted yard, past bloated horse carcasses and broken caissons, past Enfield rifles strewn about like tree branches after a storm. She looked at the Snyder place, where Martin repaired fences while Mary rounded up what little livestock had escaped the fury of the battle and the hunger of the army.

Ma said Martin wouldn't travel beyond his own property. Ma said that he had Soldier's Heart: a disease of the soul that made him skittish and moody, but Martin denied it. He said that dysentery made him unsteady, unwilling to be far from his own outhouse, and that the fatigue and sweating and palpitations were just getting used to being home. Sarah's own exhausted mind stumbled, unsteady over the thought of crossing the road and visiting. Perhaps she had some form of Soldier's Heart or mental dysentery.

Sarah looked as far down the road as she could. She prayed earnestly that Private Gemmy Smith, the crazy boy who had taken the French furlough, had made it home to Alabama safe, sound and sane.

A hollow thump brought Sarah's mind back to Pennsylvania. She felt the concussion deep in her bones. Someone was knocking on her cast. She turned and found Doctor Cunningham studying her. His smile lifted the corners of his bushy mustache but his gray sky eyes remained serious.

"How's our little nurse holding up?"

"I ain't no nurse," Sarah answered. The bitterness and exhaustion in her voice surprised even her. "I'm just a girl with a house full of wounded. I'm doing what needs doing."

"Ayup. And you are excelling at it."

Sarah wanted to argue. She didn't deserve praise for doing what had to be done. But the doctor's voice had an air of authority. If he said she was doing well, she could believe it. Knowing that someone approved of her felt as rejuvenating as three night's sleep. Sarah's heart pressed against the constraining cast.

"This past five days you and your family have seen more suffering and horror than anyone should see in a lifetime. Instead of withdrawing, the three of you have responded with compassion and dedication. Lijah's found more wounded squirreled away behind bushes and rocks than I ever thought possible. He's saved many lives. Your Mother's cooked for these men nonstop. They would have no hope of recovery without the food she provides. And you show gentle, unflinching care to your patients, even the ones whose wounds are terrible to look on. You should consider training to be a nurse."

"Ma says I'm going to be a teacher," Sarah said flatly.

His pale eyes studied her. She knew he wanted to ask her whether she wanted to be a teacher. Sarah did not know the answer. Sarah straightened, intending to get back to her letters. Her back popped so loudly she was sure he heard it.

Doctor Cunningham frowned, his mouth mimicking his mustache. "I've done all I can for the men right now. I have some spare time. Do you want me to cut off this monstrosity?"

"I can't do that. Ma'd kill me." Sarah winced, thinking of what Ma would say.

"Of course you can. It's your back and your fate, not your mother's," he answered.

"But my back . . ." Sarah's voice trailed off. She didn't even know what questions to ask. Doctor O'Neal had said that the cast was necessary. He had outlined the dire consequences of not using it. But here was another doctor calling it a monstrosity. Sarah weighed the idea of going against Ma's wishes against the freedom of going without the cast. The decision making terrified her.

"I've not read anything in the medical literature to indicate that a cast is efficacious in remediating curvatures of the spine," Doctor Cunningham said. When Sarah didn't respond, he added, "That means no one knows if the cast if going to do you any good or not."

Sarah slipped her hand into his as trustingly as a child. The Doctor's hand was not big like Pa's, but it was strong and warm and comforting. She felt his confidence spread up her arm, as if his blood was coursing through her body.

"Then cut it off, please," she said.

Sarah's feet were too anxious to walk. She wanted the cast off now, before Ma could interfere. She and Doctor Cunningham ran hand in hand through the rain like two impish children. Daisy lunged out to the end of her rope, barking furiously. Sarah barked back, then laughed at her own silliness. Sarah hadn't laughed in months. She was jubilant at the thought of bending and reaching.

They dashed into the barn. Before Sarah could think about improprieties her arms were out of her dress. Doctor Cunningham pulled the dress up and threw it over her back like a cape. He slid one hand up the side of the cast to keep from slicing her hip as he cut through the cast with his surgical saw. It was a tight squeeze.

"I don't think this is right," Sarah said. The closeness of his hand made her uncomfortable.

Doctor Cunningham looked up. His eyes were serious. "You are my patient. I have no inappropriate feelings toward you. I will stop now, if you wish."

"What in Heaven's name're you doing to my daughter?" Ma's voice boomed from the doorway. Ma stood with her fists on her hips, an angry look darkening her face. Sarah's stomach lurched, then she saw the fear in Ma's eyes. The terror made the tiny woman less intimidating. She could stand up to this. "Doctor Cunningham's freeing me."

Ma stomped within half an arm's length of the doctor. She crossed her arms over her chest in a gesture that always made Pa back down.

Doctor Cunningham didn't even notice.

"She needs that cast on account of it straightens her scoliosis and kyphosis," Ma said to him.

"Maybe it helps," he conceded, sawing away, "maybe it doesn't. I can bring you articles supporting either conclusion. But right now, this cast is causing your daughter pain. She can't bend to help the injured with this cast on. Not without bruising herself."

"Who cares about the men?" Ma spat the words.

"I care about them," Sarah said. She watched the fury build in her mother's face. She would be in for it next time they were alone.

Ma turned toward the doctor. "I ain't gonna have my daughter's life ruined because of your selfishness. She'll be warped, and all because you want her nursing your soldiers."

Doctor Cunningham finished sawing the one side and turned Sarah around so he could saw up her other side. "Sarah knows the crookedness in her back is inconsequential compared to the brokenness of the wounded. Besides, at the very worst she will be no more warped than you."

Ma turned a strange purple color. "I ain't warped." Her words came out in a gust, as if he had struck her in the stomach.

Doctor Cunningham sliced the cast along the tops of Sarah's shoulders. He grabbed the bottom edges and jerked outward. The cast cracked along her shoulders. The two halves clattered down. Sarah was free. Doctor Cunningham helped her slip her arms back into the dress that now hung loosely. The cloth, like the air, felt intense and strange against her skin. She was surprised how weak and small she felt.

"You'll need to bathe," he said. "You've been sweating inside that cast. You're none too sweet." Sarah breathed in the putrid smell. She smelled worse than the wounded.

"I ain't warped," Ma repeated, her voice a little less sure of itself.

Doctor Cunningham turned his sky gray eyes on Ma. "Does your back catch when you bend to work? Does it burn when you crawl into bed at night?"

"I work hard," Ma snapped. "Course it catches. With all I do in a day, my back should burn come evening."

"Do you have a mirror in your house? A big mirror?"

"Got one in my bedroom," Ma said. Before Sarah knew what was happening, Doctor Cunningham had Ma by the elbow. Ma clucked like a wet hen as he escorted her across the yard and up the stairs. Sarah scuttled along behind, though she did not honestly know which of the two she should protect from the other.

Doctor Cunningham looked over Ma's shoulder as he stood her in front of the mirror. He bunched her dress tight behind her so that it clung to her, revealing her figure.

"This ain't right, you in my bedroom," Ma said, flailing her arms to shoo him off.

Doctor Cunningham did not budge. "Look at your hips." His voice was level and calm and had an air of authority that allowed no argument. Not even from Ma. "Do you see, Mrs. McCoombs, how one hip is full and round and the other flat? Your spine curves, twisting the hips toward the fuller side."

"I ain't never seen that afore," Ma said in a tiny voice.

He drew a finger along her spine until he got to her shoulder blades. "It curves up here, too, making you lean slightly to the right. If your spine was straight, you'd be a good two, three inches taller."

"The women in my family's always been short," Ma's voice didn't carry much conviction.

"Ayup. Scoliosis is known to run in families."

82

"For the Lord thy God am a jealous God, visiting the iniquity of the fathers upon the children unto the third and fourth generation of them that hate me." Ma often used this verse from Deuteronomy to explain the misfortunes of people like Mrs. Snyder. She had never used it to explain problems in her own family. She turned anguished eyes to the Doctor. "I don't hate God, so what did I do to deserve this?"

"I'm a doctor, not a theologian," he said. "I don't think you deserved this any more than you deserved having a battle overrun your farm or any more than any of those men out there deserved to die."

He stared at his hands, bloodstained and beaten from the work they had been doing the last few days, then tucked them deep in his pockets. "We all have our burdens to bear. Yours is not so onerous, Mrs. McCoombs, and neither is your daughter's. I will examine her more thoroughly when I have less pressing things to do, but I suspect that she will live as productive and full a life as you yourself have." He gave her a brief nod, then fled back downstairs in a clatter of boots.

Sarah's heart went with him, joyfully skipping down the stairs after the man who had freed her. Now she could return to Mrs. Eyster's Young Ladies' Seminary. She could ride into town each day with Mary and Hans in their shackle-shimmy cart. Life would go back to normal.

But nothing was normal now, not with the war.

Ma slumped on the bed and rested her face in her hands. "Where's your Pa when I needs him?" she moaned. "This warn't how the summer was supposed to go. It don't make no sense. Ain't none of it make no sense. The Lord Almighty must be done with us."

Sarah glared at ma. Anger boiled up inside her and flashed like lightning across her eyes. She had to swallow hard to keep down the bitter words. It wasn't God's fault that she was warped: it was Ma's. Ma's, and her ancestors.

One of them had sinned a great sin and brought this crookedness upon her, maybe upon the whole nation. The months in the back brace, the pouring over the lonely books, the separation from Martin, the dead in the yard. It was all the fault of this tiny, imperious woman who looked down her nose at the whole world as if she were the most superior, when really she was the most bent, the most damaged.

"I can't wait until Pa gets back. I'll get things back to normal and you can get back to your books," Ma said.

"I'm not going back to my books. I'm not going to be a teacher," Sarah said.

Ma wagged a finger. "Now you listen to me," but Sarah stormed out the door before her mother could lay into her. Her heart drummed within her chest. This was the first time she had argued with her mother. It felt like a victory.

She bumped into Lijah, who hovered outside the bedroom door, listening. Lijah's shoulders were pinched tight up against his ears and his hands clenched in tight fists.

"I can't stand this place no more. I can't stand the fighting inside and out. I's leaving when the army leaves, whether I knows all the drum signals or no."

Sarah ruffled Lijah's blond hair until it stood on end. "I'm already missing Pa and Micah enough. I don't need you in danger, too."

"I won't be in danger. I'll be a drummer, not a solider. I gotta avenge Beatrice's death. I gotta." The freckles on his nose disappeared into wrinkles as he scrunched up his face in anger that bordered on weeping.

Sarah pressed Lijah's boney little body, all elbows and chin and shoulder bones, close to hers. She tucked his head beneath her chin and breathed in the smell of hay and sunshine in his hair.

"Eeuw. You smell like a dead horse," he said.

Sarah laughed. "Worse. Come on. There's someone I want you to meet."

CHAPTER TEN
UNWANTED VOICES

"Say hey, Miz McCoombs! You look like you lost half your weight since we last visited." Jimmy Harlow struggled to lean back on his elbows as Sarah stepped among the confederate patients who lay in the yard. He gave a smile that was half wince as he jarred his legless stump.

"I got my cast off. Look. I can sit next to you now." Sarah cradled his head against her shoulder. She tussled his wheat blond hair, just like she had done to Lijah. Jimmy melted against her in gratitude. Sarah pointed to Lijah, who glowered in the doorway, his arms crossed against his chest so that he looked like a miniature version of Ma when she was angry. "I want you to meet my brother, Lijah."

"Hey," Jimmy said

"Hey yourself," Lijah shot back. He glared at the fields, refusing to look at Jimmy. "You tricked me, Sissie. You didn't tell me you wanted me to meet no rebel."

Lijah's sullenness did not dampen Jimmy's good humor. "I seen you running through the yard. You run real fast. Bet I couldn't have beat you, even when I had me both my legs."

"Jimmy was a drummer for the 17th Georgia Infantry," Sarah said quickly so that Lijah wouldn't have a chance to say anything rude.

"Yes'm. Benning's Brigade." Jimmy's chest swelled a bit with pride.

Sarah patted Jimmy's head. She was no supporter of the Georgia Infantry, but she admired his spunk. "What made you join the army, Jimmy?"

"I joined up to get a piece o' the action. Looks like the action got a piece o' me instead." He laughed and slapped his thigh just above the amputation, then grimaced.

"But was it fun? I mean, before you lost your leg?" Sarah looked up at her brother. Lijah's eyes roved over the fields. She knew he was listening. The fear on his face told her so.

"Warn't nearly as fun as I'd thought it'd be," Jimmy replied. "I had me ideas of marching like on parade and playing fine music, but that's what I ended up doing least. I didn't figure on how much time I'd be spending hauling water, collecting firewood, rubbing down horses, cooking. Shoot, I could'a stayed home and done them chores and still had a good bed to sleep in and food to eat. I hadn't counted on the army trying to starve me to death on hardtack and chicory root coffee."

"My brother here wants to be a drummer. He says it's safer than being a soldier," Sarah said.

"Ain't no safer," Jimmy's voice turned grim. "Some of the sharpshooters, they aim 'specially for the color bearers, the drummers and the buglers. Figure if they kin take out them what rallies the men, they kin stop the whole dang line. It works, too. An' when it's all over, us in the band see the worst of it. It's us'n that carry wounded men offen the field." He sighed.

Lijah gawked at Jimmy. "What's it like, being in battle?" His voice sounded as gruff as Jimmy's had been. Sarah, sad that she had to evoke Jimmy's most painful memories, averted her eyes so her brother wouldn't see the mix of triumph and guilt in them.

"Goin' into battle? Ain't like nothing else in the world." Jimmy's eyes misted over. Sarah was not certain whether his memories were nostalgic or horrific. The look on his face was a strange mixture of love and hate, of regret and remembrance. "You reckon you're gonna be scared and you worry you'll shame yourself. But when the time comes, the fear skeddadles. All you think about is the job you got to do. And my job was drumming loud enough to keep the men going."

Jimmy pointed toward the shattered wheat field. "We was moving across there. All around me the wheat heads bowed as if big, fat drops of rain were falling on 'em. But it weren't rain what was making 'em move. It was minie balls, falling thick. We ran forward, our heads down as if running through pelting rain. And then the cannons atop the ridge, the ones we were making for, began to blast away.

"Shells, they scream. Grapeshot and canister whine. Minie balls whistle. It was like Death's band was playing, and as hard as I banged my sticks on my drum, I couldn't drown it out. Hard as I hit, my men kept going down, and I couldn't stop it."

Jimmy's voice broke. He wiped the dampness from his eyes with the back of his sleeve. "God in heaven, I drummed as hard as I could, and I couldn't drown out the sound of death. Don't 'spect I'll ever hear anything like that again. Leastways, hope not."

Lijah inched closer. His freckles showed dark against skin that had gone pallid. "Is that how you lost your leg? To a shell?"

Jimmy shook his head. "Cannonball. Leastwise, that's what I think it was. They's funny, cannonballs. They bounce along the ground, kicking up dust each time they strike. If'n ya'lls watching y'all can step aside and let 'em pass. Sometimes, though, they take a bad hop and getcha.

Last thing I remember was watching one come. I remember figuring I had to step left. Then I remember a jerk an' I was down on the ground and my leg was sticking out at a funny angle, the toes pointed opposite the knee. Tried wiggling them, and nothing happened, so I knew it was broke." He looked down at the stump. A wry smile crossed his face. "Guess I don't gotta worry 'bout wiggling them no more."

"All you need worry about now is healing yourself," said a strange voice.

Sarah had been so enrapt that a woman had come upon them without her noticing. She looked very old, with a back so hunched that her face appeared to come out of her chest. Her voice was as rusty as a barn hinge, her face wrinkled and leathery brown like the apples in the bottom of the barrel. Hair stood out from her exposed scalp in little wispy gray clumps. Her fingers, which clasped the handle of a willow basket, were gnarled, her fingernails broken and dirty. She smiled, revealing no teeth in her puckered mouth. In spite of the smile Sarah felt a shudder of repulsion run up and down her spine.

"Who're you?" Lijah said.

"You don't need to know. Now git," Ma said from the doorway. Lijah didn't need to be told twice. He took one look at Ma's glaring face and the way her arms folded across her chest and lit out for the barn as quick as his legs could carry him.

"What are you doing here, Dame Heatner?" Ma's voice would have soured milk.

Sarah gawked at the woman whom she had heard so much about but had never met. Dame Heatner was the stuff of schoolyard legends: a woman born before the War for Independence who, everyone seemed to think, was either part witch or part saint. But no one: not the schoolchildren nor their teachers, not the folks who minded the stores in town nor the ones who plowed the fields, seemed to know which.

"I came to help." Dame Heatner set her basket near Sarah. It was filled with cheesecloth packets tied up with kitchen string and it gave out a warm, green smell that reminded Sarah of autumn days.

"We don't need your kind of help," Ma said. "We don't need none of your herbs. We got a real doctor here. One that gives out real medicines."

Dame Heatner picked up her basket. "Well, I'll just ask him, then, whether he wants assistance. Where might I find him?"

"He's in the barn," Sarah said, then slapped a hand over her mouth. She leaped up and followed Ma, who was flapping her arms like an angry hen as she chased after Dame Heatner.

Doctor Cunningham looked up. His hand stopped mid-stitch in the closing of a gaping head wound as the strange parade entered the barn.

"You must be the doctor," Dame Heatner said.

"Ayup. Doctor Cunningham," he said, going back to his work.

"I'm Abigail Heatner," the old woman said. "And I am pleased to make your acquaintance. I have walked all the way from Power's Hill and brought my herbs with me. They can be a comfort for those in pain."

"Anything that will make the men feel better is welcome," the doctor said without looking up. "I won't dismiss herbs to do the trick."

"She can stay?" Ma's voice was shrill, her body tense. This wasn't the reaction she'd expected from a man with an education in modern medicine.

"Union supply wagon should be here soon with plenty of canned and dry goods, so feeding her won't be a problem." The doctor tied off his thread. He looked at Ma, studying her face with his blue-gray eyes. They seemed to soak Ma up, taking in her deepest, unspoken thoughts. Though there was no harshness, no judgment in his eyes, Sarah watched her Ma wither under the look. "Do you know some reason she shouldn't be here?"

Ma's mouth opened and closed several times but she didn't explain. Soon she and Dame Heatner were working side by side in the kitchen. They remained tight-lipped toward each other, as stiff as the boards that stood in rows throughout the fields. The men seemed as grateful for the herbal teas that Dame Heatner gave them as they were for panda, a mix of crushed hardtack and whiskey that Ma had been instructed to feed the weaker patients. Their gratitude made the uneasy truce between the two women more bearable.

"Great suppah." Doctor Cunningham scooted his chair away from the kitchen table. They had just finished a stew made from US Army peas, corn and beans, potatoes and salted beef, all from cans. A mound of food stuffs stood in the corner. The sergeant who had supervised its stacking said it was all courtesy of a government grateful for its citizen's support in helping the wounded.

Dame Heatner wiped gravy out of the wrinkles in the corners of her mouth. "Best stew I've ever eaten."

Ma blushed and peered shyly at the older woman. "'Twas the herbed dumplings what made it," she admitted. She blushed deeper as Dame Heatner offered her a toothless smile. The truce the two women had been working on all afternoon seemed cemented. Sarah breathed a sigh of relief that the kitchen would be less tense. She wasn't sure which caused it: the peace, the stew, or her bath, but she felt all weak and whoozy. It was not a bad feeling. She sighed and straightened out the folds in her dress. It felt good to wear her own clothes again.

Sarah had taken her bath right there in the kitchen while Ma and Dame Heatner clattered about, oohing over the abundance of new cans and crates. They had rigged up a curtain around the galvanized washtub, then shooed everyone else out.

Sarah had stepped into the small tub and slid into water so warm it made her skin prickle. She lathered up with the hard, harsh soap, then scrubbed with a rag until her skin tingled. It sloughed off in pale, sticky pellets. The scum left floating when she stepped out had amazed her.

"Ayup," the doctor assented. "Aftah a meal like that, I need to walk a bit. Helps the digestion." He'd no sooner said it than Lijah scraped his chair back and bounded out the door. Sarah smiled lazily after him. It was hard for a boy his age to sit still so long. She knew Lijah wasn't planning on accompanying the doctor on his walk, not unless the doctor was going east to look for the first sign of Pa.

While Ma and Dame Heatner made their rounds among the wounded, Sarah dumped scraps into Daisy's dish. The dog gulped them down. She seemed particularly ravenous as of late. It was a wonder that anyone, even a dog, could have an appetite with the stench of death and dying hanging around like a low lying cloud.

Sarah dropped the dishes into the sink and watched them fade into memory beneath the dishwater. Greasy scum rose like swirling fog on a cold, damp evening. She stared, mesmerized by the patterns. A firm hand rested on her shoulder, but she was too tired to look up.

"You look as worn out and heavy as the wash rag in your hand," Doctor Cunningham said gently. "Why don't you let me attend to these dishes? You go to bed."

"Too early," Sarah argued. "I'd never get to sleep." She didn't want to tell him that she avoided sleep and the terrible dreams that came with it.

"Then go for a walk. The evening air will do you good."

"I thought you were going on a walk yourself," Sarah mumbled. Her lips felt too heavy to form the words correctly.

"Ayup. Did. And back again."

Sarah dipped her hand into the dishwater. It was tepid. How long, she wondered, had she been standing there?

She let go the dishrag and with leaden steps went outside, where she found Lijah and Jimmy. Jimmy was sitting up, leaning against an old wooden crate. Between the boys sat a pile of pebbles. The boys took turns throwing them at an abandoned canteen. Whenever either boy hit it, it would emit a metallic thunk and the boy would crow gleefully. Beyond them, everything looked barren, lifeless. The trees in the woodlot had all their leaves shot off and looked as forlorn as they did in the dead of winter. The fields were crushed.

"The cool of the evening is good for gathering herbs." The rusty voice came from the yard. Dame Heatner had such a silent way about her that she seemed to materialize from air, appearing where nothing but twilight had been the moment before. Or maybe, Sarah thought, Dame Heatner had been there all along, but Sarah had not had eyes to see her.

Sarah felt her eyes snap open. She was awake again, alert. "Can I come? I'm interested in herbs." She followed the old woman into the fields, wondering if she could see anything in the growing dark. Dame Heatner stooped down and fingered a tiny cluster of green.

"This is tansy. Its scientific name is tanacetum. Being trampled down will make it grow so much the better. Seems the harder its life, the more determined it is to make something of itself."

She scooted sideways like a crab until she came to a whorl of fuzzy leaves. "That's mullein," Sarah said. "It'll send up a tall flower head soon."

Dame Heatner cut the leaves with her shears and laid them in her basket. "It would have, if it had time, but I need it now. Mullein, otherwise known as verbascum thapsus, induces painless sleep. It loosens the mucous. Those boys who've been shot through the lungs will want it."

"Verbascum thapsus. Tanacetum. My ma will be surprised you know the scientific names for things."

"I know a lot of things. Study a lot of books. Herbs and modern medicine aren't as far apart as your Ma supposes," Dame Heatner said.

They walked through the dusk. Sarah learned that wintergreen, or menthe, calmed stomachs. Willow, called salix by scientists, cleansed infected wounds. Agrimonia eupatoria, or common agrimony, stopped diarrhea. Learning the name and use of each new herb fortified her. Sarah dashed between plants. She was wide awake now, her cheeks flushed with the joy of discovery. Their new names sounded magical on her tongue. The more she learned, the more she wanted to know. The meadow had always been an intriguing puzzle. Now, with Dame Heatner to tutor her, it became a textbook far more exciting than Robinson's Arithmetic or McGuffey's Reader.

"Ancient physicians had a saying," Dame Heatner said. "It was 'Why should a person die when sage grows in his garden?' When things calm down I'll bring you a basket of little plants, if you like, so you can have your own garden."

"I would like that very much," Sarah found herself hoping up and down like Lijah when he expected a new lamb or calf.

Dame Heatner gave a serious nod. "And I promise to teach you what they are and what they are good for."

Even in the darkness, Sarah felt Dame Heatner's piercing eyes study her face. "Sarah, dear, your mother tells me you are studying to become a teacher."

Sarah let out a sigh. "That is what she would like me to do. But I have other plans. All I want to do is marry a farmer who'll love me and watch after me, and the two of us can stay here on the land."

"The time when women can count of that happening may be over – if such a time ever existed. Look at me. I never married, never had a man to watch after me. I had to make it on my own. It was hard. But times are changing for women. Down in Germantown the Quakers done set up a college just for women who want to learn medicine. Dorothea Dix is Superintendent of Women Nurses for the whole Union Army. Clara Barton has influenced all of Washington with her Red Cross. I hear there's a lady from Ohio, name of Doctor Mary Walker, who is a surgeon with the Union Army – and she wears pants! It's time for a woman to take her place – her own place, not a place beside her husband.

She mopped her face with her handkerchief and studied the sky, where the first stars glimmered in the velvet blue. "It's Sunday, and we've been too busy to worship. Look around you, Sarah, and thank God for what he spared."

Sarah jolted back. "You observe the Sabbath?"

"Of course I observe the Sabbath. What did you think? That just because I gather herbs I was a heathen witch? Children whispered that, back when your Mother was a girl." Dame Heatner gave with a rusty chuckle

"Why?" Sarah asked.

"Look at me. I'm no pretty picture, am I? I've been old longer than most people have been alive. But back when I was young I spurned a suitor, and then a wound on his leg festered and wouldn't heal. It wasn't witchcraft, Sarah, but it didn't matter. His pain turned to bitterness which spilled out of his mouth. An infection of the soul, you know. Such infections are very contagious. The rumors have lasted decades longer than the tongue that started them."

Dame Heatner tucked her arm through Sarah's. They picked their way toward the farmhouse. Sarah noticed a pale glow, like a yellow, burning cloud hovering over the shallow graves. She averted her eyes and pushed away the thought that she was seeing the souls of the lost.

"Eerie, isn't it?" Dame Heatner jerked her chin toward the strange light. "But it isn't anything to fear. It's methane gas. Decomposing bodies release it. I once noticed the same phenomenon in a graveyard. It set me to wondering, so I read book upon book until I learned the truth."

Sarah let out a little, nervous laugh. "I thought it was a ghost."

"You're too smart to believe in such things," Dame Heatner gave Sarah's arm a little squeeze. They had not gone much farther when Sarah noticed another pale glow. This one was beside the cowshed and it was not the ghostly, gassy glow of graves, but something white and pure. Its sweet scent wafted over the stench of death, cleansing it with the promise of new life. As she came close, Sarah realized the crooked apple tree, the one Ma had wanted Pa to cut down, was in bloom.

Ma came out and leaned against the porch post. "You see that? Too bad it's too late to bear fruit."

Dame Heatner raised her hand as if in benediction to the tree. Her voice rang with authority. "Let the earth hear, and all that is therein. For the indignation of the Lord is upon all nations, and his fury upon all their armies: he hath utterly destroyed them, he hath delivered them to the slaughter. Their slain also shall be cast out, and their stink shall come up out of their carcasses, and the mountains shall flow with their blood.

"Seek ye out the book of the Lord, and read: no one of these shall fail, no one shall want her mate: for my mouth it hath commanded, and his spirit it hath gathered them. The wilderness and the solitary place shall be glad for them: and the desert shall rejoice, and blossom as the rose. It shall blossom abundantly, and rejoice even with joy and singing."

Dame Heatner dropped her hand. She sounded tired, as if pronouncing scripture had taken the strength from her ancient body, but her words still bore the authority of the ages. They tingled up Sarah's spine, making the hair on her arms stand at attention. "Some trees are like that: it takes a shock to their system to make them bear fruit. And then they hurry, and produce in less time than anyone would expect. Some people are like that, too. And some nations."

"Listen well, Sarah Jewel McCoombs," Ma said. "Dame Heatner speaks truth."

Dame Heatner perked up. "Sarah Jewel? Is that her full name? It brings to mind diamonds. And she is that: a diamond in the rough."

"She's got a crooked back," Ma said, her voice tinged with regret.

Sarah opened her mouth, ready to defend herself, but Dame Heatner beat her to it. She placed her crook-knuckled hand against Sarah's cheek. Sarah felt her warmth on her skin.

"All of us have problems." Dame Heather said. "This girl's assets – the intellect I saw working as we gathered herbs – do you know she heard the scientific names for different plants but once and remembered them? - the compassion I've seen her use on the wounded- they far outweigh a crooked back."

Sarah smiled. They were words she'd been praying to hear.

CHAPTER ELEVEN
GIVEN AND TAKEN

"This ain't the way a Monday's supposed to go," Ma grumbled. She slapped a plate of biscuits and gravy in front of Lijah. "This war's ruined my schedule just as surely as it's ruined the wheat."

Sarah looked at the copper wash kettle Ma had placed on the stovetop. The house was a shambles of broken windows, blood streaked walls and carpets soiled beyond redemption, yet none of this rankled Ma so much as laundry day passing without the laundry getting done.

Sarah shrugged. The loss of routine didn't bother her. What was not done today could be done tomorrow. The destruction of her family's things didn't account for the emptiness in her heart. The deep and abiding loss Sarah felt was for the purity and innocence of the place. Pa could replace the broken panes with new squares of glass. He could whitewash the walls until they glowed as clean and pure as before. The furniture could be reupholstered, new carpets bought. But they would not be the same. The war had desecrated her childhood home.

It was different for her brother. Lijah didn't mourn for the comforts of home or the steady routine of farm life. Lijah missed the animals. He had still not forgiven either side for Beatrice's death.

Doctor Cunningham scraped his fork across the plate to gather up the last mot of gravy. "We won't be bothering you much longer. Jonathan Letterman, the army's medical director, is putting up a new field hospital about two miles out the York Pike. Camp Letterman's got hundreds of white tents, all in rows, and six hundred and fifty medical officers. I'll transfer my patients there as soon as I can get them moved."

"As long as you're in the area, you're to come for Sunday dinner, hear?" Ma smiled at the doctor, who went pink beneath his mustache. It amazed Sarah how quickly Ma had come to treat the doctor like one of her own. She used the same loving, scolding tone with him that she used with Pa and Lijah. Maybe he filled the hole left by Micah.

"Does that include the rebel soldiers?" Sarah asked. "Will you take them to Camp Letterman too?"

"Nope." The doctor paused to suck gravy from his mustache. "There's a hospital at Fort Henry, the Prisoner of War Camp. Confederate prisoners, when they're well enough to be moved, go there. They'll stay there until they get traded for a Union prisoner or until the war ends, whichever comes first."

Lijah gasped. "What if they's just kids? What if they's no older than me?"

Doctor Cunningham diverted his sky-gray eyes, but not before Sarah saw grief and guilt pass before them like a cloud. "Sorry, Lijah. The Army thinks that any man old enough to fight for the rebels is old enough to be punished for it."

He left for another morning of surgery in the barn. He still saw a few new cases: the less wounded, who had been pushed aside while the more dire cases were attended to.

But more and more Doctor Cunningham was treating patients whose wounds had festered. Instead of amputating shattered arms and legs, he was amputating gangrenous ones.

Sarah finished up the dishes and stepped outside. She found Lijah and Jimmy hunkered over a checkerboard. Her brother should be doing chores, but she didn't shoo him off. Work wouldn't heal Lijah's grief over the death of the broken down nag Beatrice as well as Jimmy's company would. Sarah hadn't heard Lijah say a bitter word against the rebels in days. She squatted down so she could ruffle the blond hair on both heads.

"I suppose my brother's told you about Fort Henry."

"Yes'm," Jimmy said with a smile far bigger than she expected.

"Want me to help you write a letter to your folks? They'd like to know where you are and where you're going," she asked again. Jimmy had always refused her offers with a smile, saying that a letter wasn't necessary.

"That's right nice of you, but I don't need it," Jimmy admitted. "Ain't got no family to send no letter to."

The words struck Sarah like a cannonball. How could this boy smile? Being an orphan, alone in the world, seemed a greater loss than losing a battle, or legs, or even a life. She thought of how she would feel if Ma and Pa, Micah and Lijah all died and left her. The loneliness seemed unbearable, unsurvivable. She went down, crumpling to the porch.

"No one?" she asked.

"Pa went off to war not long after Fort Sumter," Jimmy said. "He wrote regular as rain for awhile, but the letters stopped right after Shiloh. Figure he's dead. Then Ma and little ones catched themselves a fever. I nursed 'em just as good as I could, but it didn't take. I went and joined up soon as I buried the last one. Weren't nothing left at home to stay around for. Union scavengers had made off with the livestock and, what with everything' else going on I hadn't gotten around to planting' no fields."

They were silent for a while, each deep in their own thoughts. Sarah felt ashamed that she had grieved over such small losses as window panes and carpets.

"Where're you going to go, then, when the war's over?" Lijah asked.

Jimmy shrugged and ran his hand through his hair so that it stood up like a field of ripe wheat. "Ain't had cause to think about that yet."

"You can come back here," Lijah said earnestly. "You can live with us."

"I'll think on it," Jimmy said. The two boys put their arms around each other's shoulders. Sarah looked away so that they wouldn't see her tears.

The next day Ma gave Doctor Cunningham a long and earnest scolding. Afterwards, the doctor fashioned a rude crutch for Jimmy and began teaching the boy how to use it to hop around the yard. It was a terrible crutch: flimsy and too short for the boy, but the Maine doctor shrugged and said it was the best he could manage. He was a surgeon, not a carpenter. But he said that, poor piece of work that it was, it was going to do the trick for Jimmy.

All the next week Sarah watched the wounded being trundled off in the Union's creaking wagons. Every time another wagon left she saw tears of relief run hot and fierce down Lijah's face because Jimmy Harlow hadn't yet been taken off to Fort Henry. But the day came when there was only one wagon load left. Knowing how hard it was going to be for Lijah to see his new friend leave, Sarah and Ma stood on the porch with him for the leave-taking. They had their arms wrapped around each other, bookending a weepy Lijah like Weld's Grammar between Frost's History and McGuffey's Reader. Down in the yard Doctor Cunningham supervised the orderlies as they picked up litters and slid them into the back of the wagon. Jimmy stood to one side, leaning on his crutch and waiting for directions. Except for a sergeant barking orders, no one talked. The wounded looked as solemn as if they were being taken to a firing squad.

Sarah watched Doctor Cunningham suddenly stand up and pat his trouser pockets, then his jacket pockets.

"Jimmy, I seem to have forgotten my sheet of directives" he said, a frown making his mustache sag. "The doctors down at Fort Henry need to know what to do with these boys. Won't, without the directives. Can you fetch them for me?"

Jimmy Harlow brightened like a new penny. "Yessir! Where are they, sir?"

"I'll get 'em," Lijah said with a sniffle.

Doctor Cunningham waved his hand dismissively and turned back to the one-legged drummer. "In the barn. Up in the hayloft. Think you can get them?"

The brightness of Jimmy's smile wavered. "The ladder . . .?"

Sarah opened her mouth to protest. Why would the doctor want a one-legged boy to go up the ladder to the loft, especially when her brother could run the same errand much more quickly easily? But before she got a word out, Ma squeezed her shoulder tightly.

"You can do it. There's a good lad." The doctor ruffled Jimmy's hair and gave him a little pat to send him on his way. As soon as Jimmy hobbled out of sight, Doctor Cunningham walked up to the porch and ruffled Lijah's hair the same way he had Jimmy's. "And when are you marching off, young man?"

"I ain't going to war," Lijah answered with a snuffle. "I'll stand guard here, so's Jimmy can find me when it's over. And Pa. And Micah. But, Lord, the staying's so hard."

Ma squeezed her children protectively, pressing them to her. "Staying is hard. Waiting is harder than doing. But when that's what we're called to do, to do otherwise would be cowardly."

"We can find some things for you to do while you wait," the Doctor said. "You will need to help the wounded recover their skills."

"Doc, they're loaded," the sergeant called.

"Oh! And here're the directives!" With a flourish, Doctor Cunningham pulled a sheaf of papers from his breast pocket and handed them over to the sergeant, then swung up on his horse and started toward town. "Better be on your way, Sergeant. The road's rutted and you're burning daylight."

"But. . ." Lijah began, but stopped when Ma tugged him and Sarah hard into her. The carts were long gone, even their dust settled back down before Jimmy hobbled back from the barn. He looked hot and sweaty and had hay sticking out of his hair.

"I looked and looked. Cain't find no papers . . . Hey! Where's Doctor Cunningham?" Jimmy asked.

"Gone," Lijah said.

"And the wagon?"

"Gone, too," Ma said. "Looks like you missed your ride to Fort Henry and you're stuck here. But I don't keep no loafers. If'n you're staying here, you'll have to earn your keep. You two boys go hoe what's left of the corn patch. Now, get."

Ma released Lijah, who stood stock still, gaping at her. Jimmy, leaning on his crutch in the yard, had the same expression frozen on his face. Then with a whoop of joy Lijah exploded down the porch stairs and the two boys disappeared around the corner of the house.

Sarah smiled at her Ma. "Did you and Doctor Cunningham plan that?"

Ma didn't smile back. She scowled. "There's a war on, Sarah Jewell McCoombs. You think me and Doctor Cunningham would collude 'an deceive the U.S.

Government? Them's grounds for hanging." And then she winked.

The McCoombs farmhouse would have seemed empty without Jimmy. He and Lijah were constant companions, their two voices ringing brightly over the fields as Lijah trundled him around in a wheelbarrow. They patched up the stalls in the barn and scoured the fields for minie balls, whose lead could be sold for thirteen cents a pound, enough to buy new chickens. Ma set Sarah to scrubbing blood from floors and walls and sweeping up stray bandages and bits of clothing and food. Bit by bit, the house, and life itself, settled into the old routines.

That Sunday the family did not go to town to worship. It surprised Sarah, for they rarely missed church. But there was much to do around the farm and they had neither cart nor horse to take them in.

After breakfast she and the boys dragged the parlor carpet outside. They scrubbed it until the white suds turned blood-rust brown beneath their brushes. Sarah was working hard, her eyes stinging with sweat when something beckoned her to look up the Emmitsburg Road. She leaned back on her heels. Two cows trailed a distant cart that moved toward her so slowly that it raised no dust. A mountain of a man, his beard swaying in the breeze, walked between the traces where a horse should be. Sarah's heart leapt within her chest. Bent over the way he was, Sarah could not see the man's face, but the cows were Bossy and Dover.

"Pa," Sarah tried to call. Her body seemed paralyzed, her voice only a squeak. Lijah heard it and looked up, frowning at the sister who had left him and Jimmy to do all the work. His eyes followed her pointing finger. With a yelp of joy, Lijah flung his scrub brush. He ran up the road, waving his hands and hollering. He climbed Pa as if he were a sturdy tree. Pa dropped the traces and cradled his son in his arms.

"What in tarnation is going on out here?" Ma crossed the porch, wiping her damp hands on her apron. Ma's gaze followed Sarah's finger. She let out a gasp, picked up her skirts, and ran.

Sarah followed.

Ma threw herself at Pa so hard that he fell back, landing seated in the road between the traces with both Ma and Lijah in his lap. Sarah climbed atop the pile. She sobbed and buried her face in Pa's scratchy beard. They were still a blubbering, celebrating tangle of humanity piled in the road when Doctor Cunningham rode up on his roan mare.

"This is the happiest sight I've seen in months," he said with a tip of his hat and a smile that tilted his bushy mustache upward.

Lijah scrambled to his feet, spooking the roan. "Doctor Cunningham! Lookie who's here!"

"It's Pa," Ma explained. She and Sarah clambered up. They slapped at their skirts until the dust flew.

Doctor Cunningham swung out of the saddle and extended a hand to help raise Pa. "Pleased to meet you, Pa. Though I'm sure you have another name, I'm willing to bet you have none you hold so dear. I'm Elliot Cunningham."

Pa stared at the extended hand, then up the arm. He frowned and stroked his beard. "The other name's John. John McCoombs. And yes, I am prouder of 'Pa' than any other name I hold under heaven. Don't know no Cunninghams 'round here."

"I'm not from around here. Maine."

Pa frowned. "You been selling something to these women while I was gone?"

Doctor Cunningham threw back his head and laughed, exposing two rows of pearly teeth. "No, Sir! I haven't sold a thing. I'm a contract surgeon: came with the army. Your family fed me while your home was used as a field hospital. I'm here now because your wife invited me to Sunday dinner."

"He's alright, Pa. A good man. Methodist," Ma said.

Ma's word was good enough for Pa. He took the doctor's hand. It looked to Sarah like an ant hefting a grasshopper, but somehow the two men managed. The doctor handed his reins to Lijah. He took up one of the cart's traces while Pa lifted the other one, raising a squawk from the cart bed. Sarah peeked over the railings at the cage of brown chickens and the spotted suckling pigs. She held her tongue. Ma, who had always insisted on pure white pigs and chickens, wouldn't be pleased.

"Hey, Pa, where's Constance?" Lijah asked as he skipped alongside. It was another thing Sarah would have held her tongue on, for the answer was bound to be bad. If it wasn't, Pa would have had the sorrel pulling the cart and not him.

"Everything went right as rain 'til I got to the bridge over the Susquehanna," he said, grunting under the load of the cart. "There I waited in a long line while Union soldiers questioned us before letting us cross. They asked the same question of each of us: 'Is that a good riding horse?' A few answered yes, and their horses were taken from them. Most others answered that their horses never done nothing but pull a plow or cart. Some that answered that way were lying. It was clear as day, but some of the liars got away with it. Some didn't and they lost their horses anyway. I decided Constance weren't worth my soul, so I told truth and lost her."

Ma patted Pa's arm. "Better to lose your horse than your honor."

Sarah held her back a little straighter, proud to be a McCoombs.

Lijah stopped and stared at the fields. "We lost Beatrice, Pa. Rebels killed her. Or maybe Union cannon. Lord, I hope Constance wasn't here for the fighting."

"I think that's how I got my roan," Doctor Cunningham said. "Army requisition. I'm sure Constance is eating fine oats, courtesy of the Union Army."

Lijah gave the doctor a grateful look. "Still, I don't like losing her."

"Lotta people lost things," Pa answered with a ragged voice. He swabbed his streaky cheeks with the broad back of his hand. Sarah wasn't sure if it was sweat or tears he wiped away. "I heard tell a lot of it as I passed through town. The Harmons got burned out, as did Alex Currens. Both John Herbst and Alex Cobean lost their barns. William Bliss and William Comfort lost both house and barn.

"After I got over the river, I came upon a man whose fields were ripe but his help had all gone for soldiers. I harvested for him sunup to sundown for ten days. He paid me in meals and a place to sleep in the loft, and gave me some pigs and chickens to bring back."

Ma peered into the cart. Sarah held her breath, waiting for disapproval. It didn't come.

"We could use the livestock, even if they ain't the right breed." Ma gave a resigned sigh. "We got plenty damage of our own, but barn and house both stand, thank God. We'll do alright."

Sarah scanned the trampled fields and the leafless trees. Here and there, pale green promises poked tentatively through the devastation. Sarah knew her mother was right. Her gaze fell on Jimmy, sitting alone next to the rolled out parlor carpet in the yard.

"We lost plenty, but we gained some too, Pa. Come home. We've got a visitor you need to meet."

"A visitor what has need of your carpentry skills," Ma added.

After dinner Sarah watched the stars peek through faded pink clouds from her father's big porch rocker. She felt like a child, her toes just skimming the ground as she swayed back and forth. The rocker ground against the weathered floorboards, adding its deep bass to the cricket chirp and the songs of meadow frogs. Down the road the Snyder's windows glowed welcoming yellow. If she listened very carefully, she could make out Mary on the piano.

Behind her, Pa's deep voice rose, met by the lilt of her mother's laughter as she corrected a point in his story. Lijah laughed, a deep gut chuckle that made Sarah's heart soften and ache. Looking at Pa, with Jimmy on one knee and Lijah on the other, Sarah felt filled to bursting with joy. She could not imagine ever being happier than she was at that moment, and the fear that this was the high point of her life terrified her. She retreated outside, away from the happiness, holding it at arm's distance.

Maybe this way, it wouldn't hurt so powerfully when she lost it.

Footsteps crossed the doorstep and Doctor Cunningham laid a hand on her shoulder. "Do you have a beau away in the war? Is that why you are so melancholy? Or is it your brother you miss?"

His voice was as warm and comforting as his hand, but it brought nothing but sadness to Sarah's heart. These were the questions that she wanted to avoid, for they made her realize that she was not as happy as she wanted herself to believe. She was indeed melancholy, remembering what she had lost and what she might still lose. Micah hadn't written since before the battle here. It was a long silence that didn't bode well.

"I had a beau," Sarah answered. Her throat felt tight and hot and she struggled to keep a sob from choking her words. "When he came back he wasn't the same man who had left. Do you know he won't come out of his house anymore? His sister says he goes under the table if he hears a loud noise."

"He's still the same man deep inside. The war may have changed him. It's certainly changed you."

She snorted. Sarah knew he meant this to be a compliment – that she had grown capable and compassionate in the face of challenge – but all she could think about was how she and Martin had both changed. She

107

wondered if she could find it in her heart to love the new Martin – the emaciated Martin whose gaunt face and twitchy, reclusive ways reminded her of the horror and suffering of battle.

And if she did, could he find it in his heart to love the new Sarah – the crooked Sarah- who, if Doctor O'Neal was right, might die young and childless? She imagined the two of them posing for one of those fancy new daguerreotypes together.

The haunted veteran and the cripple. It was not a pretty picture.

"Ma says he has something called Soldier's Heart." Sarah wiped her face with the back of her hand and was surprised to find it slick with tears.

Doctor Cunningham gave Sarah's shoulder a little squeeze. "A lot of our fellows have that. They feel tired all the time, and their hearts race, and they can't breathe, but when we doctors examine them, we can't find anything wrong with their hearts. Nothing, at least, that a doctor can cure. Go see him. It will be healing to both of you."

Sarah turned her face away. She didn't want him prescribing healing to her. It was easier to dwell on the old dream of the handsome young couple than to think what their future might hold now.

"There you two are!" Ma's tiny shadow lay across the porch for a moment, and then was covered by Pa's enormous one. He was so big that he blocked nearly all the light from the doorway. "Come in and have a piece of apple pie made from dried apples, compliments of the US Army before Jimmy and Lijah eat it all."

"Thanks, but I saved no room," Doctor Cunningham said. "I'd best be getting back to Camp Letterman before they think I've taken a French Furlough." Doctor Cunningham shook Pa and Lijah's hands. He placed a kiss on Ma's cheek and then on Sarah's, then stepped off the porch and started for the Emmitsburg Road.

"You forgot your horse," Ma shouted.

The Doctor doffed his hat. "I didn't forget it. The words 'the Lord giveth and the Lord taketh away' are from the Bible somewhere, are they not?"

"Why Doctor Cunningham! You're almost as bad at misquoting scripture as my husband. You're quoting Job. 'The Lord gave, and the Lord hath taken away'."

"Well, the army requisitioneth and the army giveth back. Consider my roan a trade for the one you lost. I can't say whether or not it's a fair trade, but it's the best I can do."

They watched him walk down the road until he was no more than a shadow, and then that shadow blended into the evening. They stood a long while, listening to the crickets chirping cheerfully in what little tufts of grass remained. The stars passed overhead, following the same paths they had always followed.

Ma broke the silence. "Well, Sarah Jewel, we'd best get to bed. Tomorrow's Monday. We've got a mess of laundry what needs doing then."

Sarah left the rocker and climbed the stairs. Go see him, the doctor had said. But what if she did? What if he took one look at her warped back and spurned her? Sarah settled into the bed linens and tried to push the thought from her mind. She tried to focus on the laundry that needed to be done, to fill her brain with duties. But when she fell asleep, her fears became nightmares in which armless men, all wearing Martin's face, ran through the lurid fields as God's laughter crackled and boomed like thunder.

CHAPTER TWELVE
THERE IS A SEASON

"They're here," Lijah whispered, forcing Sarah from another of her confused dreams. She sat up with a start and found herself breathing hard, her skin clammy.

"Who's here? Micah?"

Lijah and Jimmy leaned in close, their blond heads bright in the moonlight, "Awe, Sarah. Micah wouldn't just sneak in home in the middle of the night."

"It's the puppies," Jimmy added. " They're here. Leastways, that's what Lijah says. I ain't been out to see, myself."

"Here where?" Sarah yawned and stretched her arms so taut that her fingers tingled. She swung her legs over the side of the bed and slipped them into the slippers Doctor Cunningham had sent to her as a birthday present.

"Out in the barn," Lijah whispered conspiratorially, "in Beatrice's old stall. Daisy was smart enough to have her puppies where Ma wouldn't find her. I think Skip must be the puppies' Pa. At least, some of 'em. They ain't all black and white like her."

"Can't be Skip's. He's been gone too long," Sarah whispered as they tiptoed down the stairs, carrying Jimmy on her hip so that his crutch wouldn't make a racket. Even with all the weight he'd gained from tucking in Ma's cooking he was still just a slip of a lad.

Skip, the Snyder's black and tan coon hound, had disappeared about the same time Hans Snyder had taken his wagon over the Susquehanna for safety. That was in late June. It was early October now, and though the war still raged far away in the south, God had been kind to the valley. He held off the frost, giving the farmers a chance to harvest a few more of their hurriedly replanted vegetables.

"Just 'cuz Skip don't go back to the Snyders don't mean he ain't around." Lijah answered with such firm conviction that Sarah wondered if he knew where Skip was.

They crossed the moonlit yard. The crickets sang their slow song of autumn and the morning star blazed low over the eastern ridge. Lijah slid his hand into Sarah's and led her into the dark barn. The warm, green smell of hay and horses had replaced the stench of rotting limbs and the tang of gunpowder and blood. Sarah thought she could still catch an acerbic whiff of the whiskey Doctor Cunningham had used once he ran out of chloroform to deaden his patients' pain. Or maybe, like her dreams, it was her memory playing tricks on her. She heard the high-pitched whine of new puppies. How strange, to have new life in a place which had so recently held so much death.

Daisy lifted her head as Sarah and Lijah squatted down in the darkened stall. Her eyes glimmered as if they caught the light of the fading stars. Her tail thudded happily a few times and she lay back among her mewling, squeaking brood. Sarah ran her hands over the six tiny forms. Five were black and white like Daisy, but the littlest was brown, with ears and eyes rimmed black like a jersey cow. Her heart told her that Lijah was right with at least one puppy's parentage. The smallest was no doubt Skip's.

Lijah scooped it up and held it protectively to his chest. "This one's my favorite. He looks like his pa."

"It's got two strikes against it," Sarah answered, preparing Lijah for what was surely to come. "One, it's the runt and two, it's the wrong color."

"But I could still ask, couldn't I? Maybe Ma would say different," Lijah said, his voice squeaky with desperation.

"Different than what?" Ma said.

Sarah nearly jumped out of her slippers. She turned and saw Ma, in her nightgown, hands firmly crossed over her chest. Even in the early morning twilight, Sarah could tell that she was scowling.

"Land sakes, you children are making an unholy noise with all your whispering and sneaking about. Loud enough to wake the dead."

Lijah held out the runt, a whimpering peace offering who let go a stream of pee at what seemed the most inopportune time. "You ain't gonna make Pa kill the runt, is you Ma?"

Ma turned away. "I 'spect we've had enough death hereabouts to last us a while. Keep it, if'n you fancy it, but don't you get yourself too attached. God has a way of weeding out the runts if'n we don't do it first."

"He's brown," Sarah interjected, just to make sure Ma wouldn't change her mind in the light of day. "Looks just like the Snyder's coonhound. The one that's missing. You know: old Skip. He's not black and white like Daisy and all the other dogs we've ever had."

"The pigs an' chickens ain't pure white 'round here no more. An' my boys ain't all Union, neither. Reckon sometimes a body has to change her ways." Ma smiled down at Jimmy as she gave him a gentle cuff about the ears.

"Thanks, Ma," Lijah said, his voice penny bright. He squeezed the pup so tightly to his chest that it yelped. "I'm gonna name him Beatrice."

Sarah stifled a giggle. Her brother might be the owner of the only male coon hound named Beatrice in the state of Pennsylvania, maybe the entire Union.

Sarah was still chuckling several hours later as she helped her ma prepare a mound of beans for canning. Ma pulled back the kitchen curtains, letting the Indian summer sun stream in. "I can't tell what in the tarnation he's up to out there," she muttered.

Sarah crossed to the window. She watched Doctor O'Neal squat in front of one of the shattered cracker crate slats that marked a shallow, temporary grave. He pulled a stub of pencil from behind his ear, licked the tip, and wrote something on a tiny notepad before lumbering to his feet and repeating the process all over again. It was unusual behavior: most of those who came to the farm were looking for missing loved ones. With the rare exception of an agent who had been paid an enormous amount to locate the son of a wealthy, prominent Southern family, dig up the body and ship it back to grieving relatives, visitors passed by the boards that marked Confederate graves.

"Got too much canning to do, or I'd go out and ask. Here, girl. Give him this and find out what he's doing." Ma thrust a glass of water into Sarah's hand and pushed her out the back door.

Sarah handed over the water and Ma's question. Doctor O'Neal stretched his back before he took a long, thirsty drink. He pulled his handkerchief from his pocket and mopped at his forehead as he glared squint-eyed at the sun.

"I'm noting the names on these boards before the sun and rain wear them away entirely. Someday, after this cruel war is over, we will notify the families, and these boys will be shipped home. Thank you for this water. It hits the spot nicely."

Ma would snort when Sarah explained what the Doctor was doing, but anything that helped rid the fields of bodies before the spring planting wouldn't be ridiculed overly much.

He handed the empty glass back, eyeing Sarah with that cautious, all-seeing look that doctors give their patients. "I couldn't help but notice that you are no longer wearing your cast, young lady. Did it disintegrate in the summer rains?"

"No sir," Sarah drew herself up to her full height. She tilted her chin up defiantly. "A Union Doctor said I didn't have to wear it any more. He cut it off me."

Doctor O'Neal shrugged. "It's your back and it's your life. I suppose we all have more important things to worry about than a little crookedness in the spine of a young girl. Now, if you will excuse me. . ." He squatted down, his back to her, and she knew she was dismissed.

Sarah passed Pa's carpentry shop, where Pa was sawing planks to make coffins. As fast as he could build a box, others dug up Union men and reburied them in land that was going to be dedicated as a cemetery next month. Word had it that President Lincoln himself was coming to give a few opening remarks. Maybe then the little town of Gettysburg could put this battle behind itself and return to the business of ordinary life.

Pa used wood from trees from Rose's Wood Lot, the little stand which stood between the McCoombs homestead and the rocky vale now known as the Devil's Den. The leaves of the trees had all been shot off during the battle. Many of the trees had never recovered. Pa laughed when he said that it was fitting for men to be buried in wood that had died the same day as they, but it was a sad laugh. The thought of it still made Sarah's heart sink.

Back in the kitchen, boiling water made the canner's lid rattle and dance, sending steam puffs into the thick, hot air like smoke signals. Sarah wiped perspiration from her face. She eyed a stack of mail on the kitchen table. She recognized Doctor Cunningham's scratchy, angular writing. He was now serving at a hospital in Washington, D.C. and wrote often. Beneath that lay another, with careful, feminine handwriting. It was addressed to the family of Micah McCoombs, Gettysburg Pennsylvania. The return address was from someone in the town of Snow Hill, in the state of

Georgia. Sarah shook her head to clear the steam and confusion. She had written enough letters to know that this letter said Micah had either died or was gravely wounded. But Micah was in Vicksburg, Mississippi. Why would a stranger in Snow Hill, Georgia write?

Sarah's voice squeaked with fear. "When'd this letter come?"

Ma loaded blanched beans into another jar. "Just now, while you was talking with the doctor."

"What's it say?"

"Don't know."

"You haven't opened it?" Sarah glared at her Ma. How could she go on canning when such an important letter lay within reach?

"It's either bad news or worse. Either way, I'd rather me and Pa learn it together, an' we both got a heap o' work to do afore we can sit and think on hard things. Here, you take Pa this lunch. But don't tell him none that'd upset him." She held out a basket covered by a red and white checked cloth that matched her blotchy face.

Sarah stared at the dampness on Ma's cheeks, angered that it came from canning, not crying. She jerked the basket from Ma's hands. "Well, I just may tell Pa. Some things are more important than keeping on schedule."

"I'll deal with your sass later," Ma shouted, but the back door banged shut on the words.

The air in the carpentry shop was warm and rich with the smell of wood shavings. Sarah dusted sawdust from a corner of the bench and set down the basket. She pulled back the cloth, revealing two cheese sandwiches and a canning jar of water. Three very small but very sweet apples, part of the first harvest ever from the crooked tree, nestled in the basket's curve.

Sarah picked up a board and sited down it. It corkscrewed, twisting like a spiral staircase. "Some of this lumber isn't good for much more than firewood," she said.

"Some of it has so many minie ball holes it seems natural only for peg board," Pa grunted. "I use what I can. I'd be a sin to waste it."

"Why does this one curve, Pa?"

Pa squinted as he studied the board. He took a bite from his sandwich and chewed it contentedly before he answered. "Who knows what makes a board to warp. Most time, I 'spect it was cut wrong to begin with. Ain't no fault of the board if its maker cut it wrong."

"But you can straighten it, can't you? For as long as I can remember, you've fixed things. A broken wheel on my baby buggy, a skinned knee: you could fix it all."

She looked at the sadness in his gentle brown eyes and felt her confidence slip.

"Ain't no man alive what can straighten that board."

Sarah's throat tightened. "Why's that?"

Pa shrugged his big shoulders. "That's just the way of the world, I 'spect." He took another bite of sandwich and sighed. Flies buzzed in and out of the open door, lending a somnolent drone to the air. Sarah felt suddenly drowsy. The warmth of the air and the sound of the flies lulled her toward thoughtlessness. She blinked her eyes tightly, afraid to lose her train of thought on what seemed like the verge of something important.

"Why does God allow some things to go crooked, Pa?"

"I reckon so He can get the glory for straighten 'em out. It says in Jeremiah somewhere that He will make the rough places smooth and the crooked, straight."

"There you go misquoting scripture again. That's from Isaiah," Ma said as she entered the shop. She fixed Sarah with a nervous glance. "You told him yet?"

Sarah shook her head. Ma seemed to regain her power. She crossed her arms over her chest and glared at the drifts of sawdust in the corners. "Don't you go eating in here with all the shavings. Come into the sunshine. It's healthier there."

They settled onto a log in the protective shade of the crooked tree. Sarah breathed in the sweet scent of apples hanging like dusky jewels among leaves translucent in the noon sun. Ma called Lijah by name and the boy's head shot up and hovered over the crest of the green hill. When he ran, Jimmy followed closely on the two sturdy crutches that Pa had made.

"We got us a letter," Ma patted the pocket of her apron as Lijah and Jimmy clambered onto Pa's lap. Sarah held her breath as Ma withdrew the paper from its creamy envelope and smoothed it flat. She held it out at arm's length, tilting her head back to get the best angle on it. "Says here Micah was shot in the stomach during the battle for Chickamauga Creek."

Sarah grabbed Pa's workbench to keep herself from toppling over. She knew that a gut shot meant certain death. She herself had seen too often that what the bullet didn't accomplish, the fetid mix of stomach bile and blood would.

It was deathly quiet in the workshop as the family digested the news. Finally Ma squinted over the top of the letter at her husband. "I don't recall Micah's name being on the list of wounded writ up in The Compiler, do you, John?"

"Reckon they can't keep track o' all the boys," Pa answered.

Ma nodded, accepting Pa's answer. "The girl what wrote this took care of him for a morning in her farm house, 'fore a Union wagon evacuated him to Chattanooga. Trust our army to do it right and not leave boys laying about wounded in enemy territory."

"They wouldn't move him if'n they didn't think he was going to recover," Pa said.

Sarah nodded, remembering the wounded who'd been left behind to die when the Confederate Army abandoned her own farm. Perhaps there was hope.

Ma continued reading. "She says she was real affected by how polite and gentlemanly he was, so she had to write."

Sarah thought of First Lieutenant Sheldon Freeborne, who was more gentlemanly than Micah had ever hoped to be. But gentlemanliness had not saved him. Nor had it saved Micah. If Micah was still alive, something else, luck or fate, or the hand of God, had plucked him from destruction. Sarah grabbed the red and white checked napkin from the lunch basket and pressed it to her face, fighting back tears.

"There, there, Pa." Ma put her scrawny arm over Pa's broad, quaking shoulders. "I 'spect we'll hear from him soon."

Pa gave a mighty sniff. It set Sarah to sobbing. Pa pulled her tight, folding his arms around her and her brother and Jimmy and Ma. Sarah felt his strength and her mother's determination and her brother's hope and Jimmy's optimism spread through her until the McCoombs family was one body suffering from the loss of its one missing member.

"Aren't you the picture of familial love and harmony?" Dame Heatner's voice pulled them apart from each other.

"We got news from Micah. He's wounded but we expect he'll heal. Have an apple," Ma held out one of the little gems.

Dame Heatner took it and studied it a moment, joy folding the wrinkles of her face one into the other and exposing her toothless gums. She rubbed it on the bosom of her blouse until it cast back the sun diamond bright. "I know someone who thought that tree would never amount to anything."

"Some of us had faith," Pa said with a happy snort. He elbowed Ma, nearly sending her over sideways.

Ma jostled Pa back good-naturedly. "Some of us had excuses when it came time to cut down that tree. Sometimes I'm glad folks round here don't treat my words as gospel truth."

Dame Heatner handed a bundle of herbs to Sarah. "I'll trade you eupatorium perfoliatum, commonly called boneset, for this apple. I brought it for your new herb patch.

It'll treat fevers and flu. The superstitious among us, of which I am not counted, believes it drives away evil spirits and negativity."

The roots were damp and had clumps of good, dark soil clinging to them. Sarah held the bundle to her nose and breathed in the heady smell while Dame Heatner reached into her basket again, this time bringing out a worn, but clean copy of Weld's Grammar. The McCoombs family's copy had been too blood-soaked to save.

"That for me?" Sarah's heart dropped. In the months since the battle she had been too busy setting the farm to rights to study. She still was not ready to resume.

"No, Sarah Jewell. For me." Ma's face reddened. She snatched the book from Dame Heatner and tucked it away in her apron pocket with the letter from Georgia. "You know, what with this war dragging on, there's a shortage o' teachers. Dame Heatner an' I have been talking on it, and she thinks if'n I work on my grammar, I might just pass the exam, old married lady that I am. I always wanted to be a teacher."

The idea struck Sarah like a thunderbolt. All those months of hard study were to fulfill Ma's dream for herself. She glared at her mother, livid with the thought that Ma had her own wishes to fulfill. She felt used. "What about me, Ma? What am I supposed to do?"

Ma put her arms around Sarah and squeezed. This time, the hug wasn't for the McCoombs family, but for Sarah alone. It was tight and strong, with all the assurance that Ma's bandy, muscled arms could muster. "If there's one thing I've learned about you through these past hard months, Sarah Jewell, it's that you're strong. You can do anything you want to, crooked back or no. You don't need no Ma telling you what's right for you. Go back with Mary to Mrs. Eyster's Young Ladies' Seminary, if'n you want. I ain't got a doubt that Doctor Cunningham would recommend you for nurses training, or even medical school, if'n that's what your heart says to do. There's women brave enough to do that now, I hear. Whatever you do, it'll be your choice, not mine."

Her choice. These past months, nothing that Sarah had done had really been her choice. Like a reed in the wind, she moved with the rush of events, bending to the tasks at hand. Everything she had done had been a matter of necessity, dictated by difficulties. She had not chosen to wear the body cast, nor drop out of school. She had not chosen to dress wounds and write letters and scrub gore from the family carpets. But these things had needed doing, and she had done them. The hurricane had passed over and left her, bent but not broken, amid the peace of a loving family and a healing land.

Somewhere the storm continued. The war raged, ripping lives apart and scattering dead and wounded in its wake. Here, there was love and the promise that things would go back to normal. Sarah looked about her at new grass growing in the fields that had been churned by wagon wheels and watered with blood. By next summer the fields would look as if nothing unusual had ever happened here. Could her heart heal as well? Could she return to her past dreams?

"I don't want to be a nurse," Sarah said with conviction. "And I don't want to be a teacher either. What I want is to study herbs and learn how they can help healing."

"Old wive's tales," Ma muttered.

"No. Pharmacology," Dame Heatner said. "It's a whole new area of study."

Ma looked impressed with the scientific-sounding word. "Pharmacology," she said, enunciating each syllable with due reverence.

"Pharmacology," Sarah repeated. She had never heard the word before, but she liked the sound of it. Doctor Cunningham would know where a young lady might inquire for admittance into a school of Pharmacology. She would go and ask him tomorrow.

Sarah brushed the apple leaves from her skirt. She held her head high and her back as straight and tall as she could. She plucked a sprig of peppermint from her new herb garden and sniffed its fresh, bright scent before walking out to the Emmitsburg road. Many choices lay ahead. Her first was to tell Mary the news about Micah. Her second choice was to see how Martin was faring. She'd heard he suffered from terrible dreams that left him shaken and frightened. Peppermint could help that.

Maybe he would feel well enough to go with her to see President Lincoln when he came to dedicate the new cemetery next month. But the decision, of course, would be his. Whether or not he went, Sarah knew she would go. Her decision was already made.

ALSO BY JENNIFER BOHNHOFF

CODE: ELEPHANTS ON THE MOON

Available in paperback and ebook at your favorite online booksellers.

"And now some special messages," the radio announcer said. "The siren has bleached hair. Electricity dates from the twentieth century. The moon is full of elephants."

Elephants on the moon doesn't make any sense to Eponine Lambaol, but little has since General Petain, the leader of the French government, allowed the German army to occupy half of France in the spring of 1940. She doesn't understand why she and her mother left Paris for this small, provincial town near the coast of Normandy, or why the natives seem to hate them even more than they hate the Germans. She wonders where her father is and what is he doing. She doesn't understand why some French support the Germans while others support the maquisards, the underground army sabotaging the occupation forces. Is anyone - even her own family - worthy of trust? And what about the charming, handsome son of the mayor? He's hard to resist, but is he on the wrong side?

As rumors of an allied invasion swirl around her, Eponine begins to understand that nothing and no one is what it seems, and that the phrase 'The moon is full of elephants' makes more sense and is fraught with more danger than she could have ever believed possible.

ABOUT THE AUTHOR

Jennifer Bohnhoff is a middle school teacher, cross country and track coach. She is also the athletic director for the Albuquerque chapter of Team RWB, an organization that seeks to use exercise and social activities to help veterans reintegrate into civilian life and she sings in the choir at Faith Lutheran Church. But what she loves most of all is helping people reach that "ah hah" moment when they suddenly understand the connections between themselves, the past, eternity, and the world around them. She tries to do this with music, movement, writing, teaching and simply living.

Mrs. Bohnhoff is the mother of three handsome men, the mother-in-law of two beautiful daughters and the grandmother of one very smart granddaughter with another on the way. She lives in Albuquerque, New Mexico with her husband and a petulant stinker of a cat who cares nothing for her writing.

Made in the USA
San Bernardino, CA
22 August 2014